D1368423

And All That Madness

ISBN:10: 1-4802-7898-X
ISBN 13: 9781480278981

And All That Madness

Joan Merrill

Also by Joan Merrill

And All That Murder (iUniverse, 2009)
And All That Sea (iUniverse, 2010)
And All That Stalking (CreateSpace, 2011)

THANKS

Dian Kiser, Pamela Rains, and Carol Sloane for their valuable critiques.

Rachel Dory for another fabulous cover.

Chapter 1

"CASEY, I JUST found out. Georgia Valentine didn't kill herself. She was murdered." Dee's excited voice echoed in my ear.

I'd been doing background checks for my bread-and-butter client, the Barton-Lehman law firm, and had a hard time switching from the byzantine pathways of cyberspace to Dee's fantasy world. "Dee, what are you talking about?"

Dee's tone had a touch of sarcasm. "Georgia Valentine, you heard of her, right?"

"Yeah, along with Duke Ellington and Miles Davis." I replied in kind. Georgia Valentine was America's first and most influential female jazz singer, known not only for her unique approach to songs, but also for her drug addiction.

Dee said, the irony gone. "You know she died of a heroin overdose?"

"Who doesn't? But I thought you said 'murder'?"

Dee sighed. "I did. This letter of hers, someone found it, says she was clean when she died. Someone else gave her that shit." She paused for emphasis. "Someone killed her."

"Right. And Marilyn Monroe was murdered by the Kennedys, Elvis really isn't dead, and JFK was shot by, fill in the blanks." I scoffed. People hated to think their idols died by ignominious means, so they invented conspiracy stories.

"Now, Casey, listen to me. This is for real. This musician, name of Bobby Walton, just passed. They went through his things and found a letter from Georgia. She wrote him she was off drugs. But get this, she told him someone was out to get her and she was scared."

"Scared? Of what?"

"That someone was gonna do away with her."

I got up from my desk, holding my phone to my ear, and headed for the kitchen. I needed some coffee to deal with this conversation. "Why would anyone want to do that?"

Dee sighed. "I don't know. But Georgia lived in a fast world, working in clubs owned by gangsters, hanging with drug dealers, being with low-life men. It could be anybody."

I grabbed my coffee beans from the cupboard and shook some into the grinder. "But history says -"

She snorted. "Screw history. What do those people know? They didn't live the life."

Dee Jefferson had been a singer with the King Basington Orchestra at the tail end of the Big Band Era, struggled through the lean years after the Beatles took over, and ended up owning a jazz club in San Francisco's North Beach. I lived a few blocks away in Chinatown and considered her club my second home.

I held the little grinder close to my body to muffle its sound. "But, Dee, be reasonable. Don't you think if someone had killed her, people would know about it? It's an accepted fact she died of an overdose. Which is not hard to believe, given she *was* an addict."

"What's that noise?" She sighed. "You and your coffee. Well, some people *do* doubt she done it herself. They think it was murder. I've heard those rumors for years."

I put the ground coffee into my espresso maker and turned it on.

"Really? From whom? Were they reliable sources?" I sounded like a television pundit, for crissake.

"Yeah, other musicians, cats who knew her, worked with her."

I stared at my espresso machine, willing it to hurry up. "But how come these rumors never surfaced? How come the critics -" Her har-rumph sounded in my ear. "Dee, you can't ignore the facts. Everything ever written about Georgia Valentine says the same thing. She died of a self-administered overdose, period."

Dee let out a sound that can only be described as derisive. "Maybe they never had the evidence to prove anything different. But this letter -" She trailed off.

I took a deep breath. "Dee, let me ask you a question. What's your interest in all this? Why would you want to open this can of worms?"

She was silent for a few moments. When she spoke, she used a softer tone of voice. "I guess it's 'cause of what Georgia Valentine meant to me and other black women. She came into this world with three strikes against her, poor, black, with a teenage mother and no father. But she had talent and rose up. Way up. Sure, she took drugs, mainly to cope with all the shit that went down then. The po-lice hounded her, hoping to bust her. She spent a year in jail and then couldn't work in New York. She gets clean and instead of getting some credit, some creep shoots her up and she fell back into the gutter again. She's gone down in history as someone who gave in to drugs. Forget all her suc-cess. That bugs me more than I can say."

My coffee was ready. I poured it into a mug and carried it over to my chair by the window. I'd rarely heard Dee so poignant. "Okay," I sighed. "Tell me more about the letter."

Dee spoke rapidly. "Like I said, it was in Bobby Walton's trunk, in his attic. They found his letters and other stuff. His son didn't even read nothing, just turned it over to the New York Jazz Society. And Freddy, you remember him from the cruise?" She took a deep breath, while I murmured my assent. "Well, he belongs to the Society and, when he heard about the trunk, he went through it and found the letter. Georgia'd written Bobby for years, but he only kept this one letter. Probably because of what she said about a threat." She paused. "Anyway, Freddy's not sure what to do about it. He remembered you, how you found the Countess when she went missing from the ship, so he wants your advice."

I took a sip of coffee. "I see."

No matter how crazy I thought her idea, I owed it to her as a friend to treat it seriously. "Okay, I would say the first thing to do is authenticate the letter, see if it was really written by her."

"Well, Freddy says it's definitely from her, the things she said -"

I used my professional tone of voice. "Nevertheless, if you are really serious, this is what you have to do."

"Okay, I got it. But how do we do it?"

The phone pressed against my ear, I gazed down at the scene below, buses, cars and people moving purposefully along Stockton Street. "First you get a piece of her handwriting the law will accept, a written contract, for example, and then get a handwriting expert to compare it with the found letter."

"Okay, that sounds simple enough. How do I find a handwriting expert?"

"Ask somebody."

"Who?"

"You'll have to find the right person to ask."

"How?"

We were going around in circles. "Get an expert."

I expected her to ask "Who?" again and we'd be doing our own version of the old Abbott and Costello "Who's On First?" routine.

But she fooled me. "I know what I need."

"What?"

"A private detective."

Oh, oh. I should have known. Last year, she asked me to look into the supposed suicide of a friend of hers and it turned out to be serial homicide. Then while we were on a cruise, she recommended me to find a missing passenger. And just a few months ago, she involved me in finding the guy who was stalking and murdering young jazz singers.

And here she goes again, trying to get me involved in another homicide. Only this time it was a fifty-year-old cold case involving one of the best known icons of American culture. Jesus, I'd never be out of work so long as Dee is around.

Chapter 2

By THE TIME I got to the club, it was almost seven. Dee's was on Green Street in San Francisco's North Beach. It was my hang and had been since I'd first wandered in there seven years ago. I was a private investigator with a passion for jazz singing. I was lucky to have found Dee Jefferson, who was a friend as well as a damned good singer.

The music hadn't started yet and the joint was pretty full for a week night. Luckily, I didn't have to find a seat, because Harry was at his usual table and I always sat with him. He came to Dee's after work on weeknights, except for Monday 'cause he didn't like big bands. He read *The New York Times*, ate one of the six dishes on the menu, and stayed for the music. He loved to hear about my cases and was the ideal sounding board, attentive, logical and supportive. Sometimes when I was really lonely, I fantasized about marrying him, but he was sixty and a confirmed bachelor.

"Did Dee tell you about the Georgia Valentine letter?" I asked as I sat down, sliding into my chair before he had the chance to stand.

"Huh? Georgia Valentine? Letter? No, she didn't. She's been busy."

Dee served as hostess on the nights she didn't perform. I glanced around and spotted her, which was easy since she always wore red. She was on the other side of the room chatting with customers.

I turned back to Harry and spoke in a low voice. "A friend of hers got possession of a letter from Georgia Valentine written fifty years ago. Dee says it proves she was murdered. She wants me to investigate."

Harry's eyes grew wider with every word. "Good grief. She doesn't want much, just a rewrite of history."

Rae, Dee's longtime waitress, came over and, seeing that Harry was still nursing his Campari and soda, asked me if I wanted a draft or a glass of white wine. I ordered wine and asked Harry what he wanted to eat. We decided to share a Caesar salad and an order of fried calamari.

"But you know, Harry, Dee may not be that far off. I've heard rumors Georgia may have been killed."

His eyes narrowed. "But with what motive?"

I shrugged. "Could be any number of them. Jealous boyfriend. Unpaid debt to a dealer. Cover up. That wouldn't be unheard of."

His expression was grave. "But, if that's what happened, why haven't we heard about it before now?"

"Because people tend to believe the authorities. Watergate, Iran-contra, weapons of mass destruction, Ponzi schemes that bring down an entire economy. I could go on, but you get the picture. Who's gonna contradict the police in a case like this? A known drug addict takes an overdose. Who'd question it?"

Rae brought my wine. Harry waited to speak until she had gone. "Yeah, you're right. But people use that same argument to accuse the government of covering up such things as a visit from aliens from outer space and orchestrating Nine Eleven. Some of the government's supposed conspiracies are ridiculous. Maybe this is another example of a refusal to accept the facts."

"Well, could be. But it's not that far-fetched. Imagine this, Georgia's in the hospital. There's absolutely no security. Anyone can come into her room. A guy wearing a white coat enters, sticks a needle in her arm and splits. Who's gonna stop him? Not even Georgia. Later they find her dead, a needle and an empty packet by the bed. They figure one of her visitors slipped her the stuff and she shot herself up. They assume it because she was an addict."

Harry rubbed his chin. "Hmm, okay, I admit that's plausible." He took a sip of his drink and made a face. He hated the taste of Campari. He claimed he only drank it so he wouldn't become an alcoholic. "Tell me more about the letter they found. How does it prove she was murdered?"

I leaned closer to him. "Well, I haven't read it, just heard about it from Dee's friend. Georgia said she was happy to be off drugs, but was afraid someone was out to get her. Unfortunately, she didn't say who it was."

Harry frowned and opened his mouth to reply.

I leaned back and held up my hands. "Before you say anything, I realize she could have been paranoid. It's a fact she was hounded by the narcs. They were always hanging around, hoping to catch her with drugs so they could lock her up again. She had a reason to be afraid."

Harry made a face. "Yes, the Feds had enormous power in those days and kept an eye on anyone who was well-known."

"Dee says jazz musicians were considered low-life drug addicts who played a crazy kind of music. And don't forget, most of them were black. Not the kind of people the Feds liked."

"Yes, jazz musicians were in the class with homosexuals and communists, two of Hoover's favorite targets."

"Yeah, so is it so hard to believe they wouldn't give a damn how Georgia Valentine died? And if it smelled of murder, they'd look the other way?"

Harry sighed. "No, I guess not." He looked me in the eyes. "So are you going to take Dee up on her offer?"

I met his gaze. "You know, I think I just might. I've kind of talked myself into it."

Chapter 3

I'D FINISHED MY run, showered, and had my breakfast. Nothing to do now but get to work.

That meant walking over to my computer desk in the corner of my living room. I lived in a one bedroom apartment in a four-unit building next to the Stockton tunnel in Chinatown. The landlady, Mrs. Wong, and the other tenants were Chinese. Some people would think it strange, a white woman living in an all-Chinese neighborhood, but I wanted to live where I could walk everywhere. And this apartment was perfectly located, near North Beach, the Marina, the Embarcadero, and downtown. And it had a garage where I kept my Mini, the smallest car I could find. It suited me perfectly. Besides, I adored Chinese food.

I had my own agency, McKie and Associates, although the latter were non-existent, and worked from home. If I had to meet a client, we either rendezvoused at his office or at a neutral location, such as Victoria's Bakery down the street. I didn't want people to know where I lived. Not the kind of people I dealt with.

I did private investigations, mostly background checks for Barton-Lehman. Occasionally I was hired for something juicier, such as fraud, a missing person, rape or homicide, which, I had to admit, I found far more interesting than computer searches. But without the latter, I wouldn't survive.

So all in all, I was pretty happy, my only problem being a mild case of Baby Anxiety. I would be thirty-seven my next birthday and didn't want to remain childless forever. I had a fairly new boyfriend, Aaron Klein, who lived in New York. But I seriously doubted he'd be the one to solve my problem. I had a Plan B, which involved going to a sperm bank, but wanted to keep it as a last resort. A very last resort.

But I had a few years before having to make that decision, so I immersed myself in my work. And I think the Georgia Valentine case was gonna be interesting, murder or not.

Dee had given me Freddy's number. I punched it in, hoping to catch him at home. Freddy Clarke played trumpet for the current version of the Basington band. He and Dee had a thing going back when Dee was with the band, which had been rekindled on the cruise. But when we'd reached port, Dee declared an end to it. She's a "been there, done that" kind of gal. She didn't like to repeat herself, especially when the first time around hadn't been all that great.

I lucked out. Freddy answered and I identified myself. After a little reminiscing about the cruise, we got to the point.

"Dee tells me you have a letter supposedly written by Georgia Valentine."

"Yeah, and I don't know what to do with it."

"What do you mean by 'do with it?' "

Freddy cleared his throat. "I mean I don't know if I should tell someone about it, like the cops. The people who found Bobby Walton's trunk gave it to the New York Jazz Society, and I'm the president. Bobby's got no kin, so it's up to me to act on it."

I started to pace my tiny living room. "What does the letter say exactly?"

"Jeez, I read it so many times, I know it by heart. She says she's been sick. That ever since she got out of jail, she'd been clean. 'I ain't took no damn dope,' she says. Then she says she'd been working in theaters 'cause I can't work in no damn club because they took away my damn cabaret card.' But here's the part that bothers me, she says 'Bobby, I'm scared, I think they're trying to get me.' But she doesn't give any names. When I told Dee about it, she got all excited. She says

10

it just proves what everybody's always suspected, someone gave Georgia the drugs. She didn't take them herself."

He paused.

I figured he expected me to say something. "And what do *you* think?"

He sighed. "I dunno. It was a long time ago. Even if it's true, what could anyone do about it now?"

"Well, people do investigate cold cases. And sometimes they find that people who've been convicted of a crime are actually innocent. This would be the opposite, an accidental death that turned out to be a homicide."

"But do you think it's possible to solve a case that old?"

I laughed. "That's the big question. I don't know. You'd have to find evidence and that would be extremely difficult after such a long time."

"But could it be done?"

"Anything's possible. People are still looking into the Jack the Ripper murders and that was over a hundred years ago."

Freddy rubbed his chin. "What do you think I should do?"

"Well, as I told Dee, the first thing to do is authenticate the letter."

"You mean see if it was really written by Georgia?"

"Yes."

He raised his brow. "Could you do that?"

"Yes, if I were paid. Handwriting experts are expensive."

He cleared his throat. "Well, the Society has money for grants, and I think this would be a good one. So can I hire you?"

"Sure. What you want me to do is see if the letter was actually written by Georgia Valentine, yes?"

"Yes."

I pressed him. "Nothing else?"

"Nope, first things first." He meant first we see about the letter, then the supposed murder.

"Okay, that sounds easy enough. Here's what I suggest. Copy the letter. Place the original in protective cover and put it in a safe place, like a safety deposit box. Then when I locate the handwriting expert, I'll tell you where to send or bring the original. Okay?"

"Got it. But we may ask you to go on to stage two."

"Which is?"

"See if Georgia Valentine was murdered."

I sighed. "As you say, first things first."

I made another cup of coffee and took it over to my easy chair by the window. The sun was reflected in the windows of the building across the street, brightening my mood. I looked forward to this new assignment. It wouldn't take me long to complete the letter authentication. All I had to do was acquire a sample of Georgia Valentine's handwriting and arrange for an expert to compare it to Bobby's letter. Piece of cake.

It was morbid of me, but I hoped they'd want me to go on to stage two, to see if Georgia Valentine was murdered. Now *that* would be just what I needed right now, a challenging case.

As I gazed out at the traffic above the tunnel, I thought about how to proceed. As I mentally went through my options, I remembered by former boss, Pat O'Halloran.

When I quit the Oakland Police Department fifteen years ago, I found a job with Pat's agency in San Francisco. After eight years, he decided to move to Arizona and asked me if I wanted to buy the business. I jumped at the chance. I loved the work, especially the cases we worked on together, like catching the serial rapist in Santa Rosa. For that one, I'd gone undercover and I had to admit it was kind of fun masquerading as a street walker, kind of like going to a Halloween party. But I was well aware of the realities of a streetwalker's life. It was difficult and dangerous. But for one night, it was interesting. I didn't, of course, get into a car with a john. I wasn't that brave. Or that stupid. But, by talking to the girls, I got the information we needed to ID the guy.

Pat had established a forensics accounting firm in Tucson and was happy to be dealing with white collar criminals instead of scumbags. I imagine he'd had occasion to use a handwriting expert and could recommend one. I put a call into his office and got a recording. I left a message, explaining what I was looking for.

Then I moved over to my computer, where I checked to see where Georgia Valentine's papers were located. They were at the Josef Katz Jazz Collection in New York. I called there and explained I wanted a copy of one of Georgia Valentine's letters or contracts in order to authenticate her handwriting. I explained I was a licensed investigator working on behalf of a client. I figured that was all they needed to know. They seemed to accept that and named the search fee. I asked them to set the process in motion. My work completed for the day, I had a few hours before it was time to go over to Dee's. I decided to do some research on Georgia Valentine to get a head start on stage two just in case it came to that. Her life was well-documented, so it didn't take me long to get her biography.

Georgia Valentine was born on March 7, 1918, in Harlem, to a fifteen-year-old single girl. With no chance of marriage to the father, who wasn't even out of high school, the young girl did her best to raise the child. She lived with her mother, who worked as a housecleaner.

One of Georgia's relatives, a distant cousin, raped her when she was eleven, an experience that left a permanent scar on her psyche. In a few years, she went to work cleaning and doing odd jobs in a brothel. Later, people said she had performed more intimate tasks, but she and her mother always denied it. She got her first singing gig in a small local bar. That led to more jobs and she was eventually "discovered" by an entrepreneurial type who figured he could make money off her talent.

He was the first of a series of unscrupulous men who exploited her. Georgia, who was beautiful as well as talented, accepted these relationships with enthusiasm, interpreting the men's interest as something deeper. With each "partnership," her star rose until she reached what many would have considered a desirable position, the most sought after and highest paid jazz vocalist in the business.

However, as a black artist in those pre-Civil Rights days, she was treated with less than respect, forbidden to enter by the front door of the club where she performed. Or not allowed to mingle with the all-white audience who came to see her.

When she toured for a time with a popular white band, she was frequently refused accommodation at a hotel or restaurant where the white band members were welcomed. The accolades did not make up for these slights and she never ceased to suffer from insecurity. To ease her anxiety, she used booze and drugs until she spent a year in prison and got clean.

Supposedly.

Chapter 4

I GOT TO the club exactly at six, opening time. I knew Harry would be there soon, and I was hoping Dee would have time to talk about the Valentine case.

As I sat down at Harry's table, I spotted Dee just entering the club through a door next to the bar. She had an apartment upstairs, which had both an outside and inside entrance. I don't think many people knew about it.

As I caught Dee's eye, I waved her over.

"Whassup?" She asked as she joined me. "Find out anything about the letter?"

"Only its contents. But I've got the ball rolling." I explained about talking to the Joseph Katz Jazz Collection and my friend Pat. "But I wanted to talk to you about some stuff I read about Georgia."

Her brow raised in question. "Ye-s-s-s-s?"

"I knew she was an addict. That's common knowledge. But I didn't know how much the Feds pressured her. It sounds like they harassed her big time." Dee nodded vigorously. "Why did they do that? And how did they get away with it?"

"Away with what?" Harry had arrived and slipped into his chair opposite us. "What have I missed?"

I smiled at him. "I was reading about Georgia Valentine and I'm shocked about how much time and energy the Feds spent trying to bust her. They searched her every chance they got, her handbag, her dressing room, her apartment, sometimes without warrants. How could they do that?"

"Hah!" Dee's tone was sharp. "Now you know why black folks don't like the po-lice."

"But why pick on Georgia Valentine? She wasn't a threat to the government."

"'Cause she was famous and successful." Dee sneered. "The po-lice didn't like it when black folks got uppity."

Rae placed our drinks on the table and moved off to the next customer.

Dee said. "It wasn't only Georgia they were after. It was Miles, Bird, Dexter Gordon, Stan Getz, Chet Baker, and plenty more, all the greats. You wouldn't believe how many cats they put in jail."

I looked at her. "Was it because they were jazz players or black?"

She snorted. "Both. Do you know they even arrested Ella Fitzgerald, who never used an illegal drug in her life?"

I stared at her. "Come on. I don't believe it."

Dee's tone was indignant. "I'm telling you the truth. When Ella was doing a gig in Houston in the late Fifties I think it was, the vice squad came storming into her dressing room with guns drawn."

Harry's eyes widened with surprise and curiosity. "Good grief. Looking for drugs?"

Dee continued. "Yeah. But all they found was Ella and her assistant drinking coffee and eating pie. But a couple of musicians, Dizzy Gillespie among them, were shooting dice, so they arrested the whole bunch for gambling."

"You're kidding." I continued to stare at her. I had a hard time believing this story. "And what happened?"

"Well, as soon as the concert producer, none other than Norman Granz, heard what was going on, he marched into the dressing room and confronted the police. The musicians and Norman were taken down to the station. Granz paid the bail and got everyone back in time for the second set." Dee sat back in her chair, crossing her arms across her chest.

"Good grief. I never heard that story." Harry interjected. "Why on earth would they raid Ella's dressing room? She wasn't known as a drug taker, was she?"

Dee let out a short laugh. "Hell, no. She was as straight as they come. People say it was a set up. They were hoping to find drugs and probably would have planted them if Granz hadn't showed up like he did."

I asked Dee. "Just so they could brag about busting a famous jazz artist?"

She nodded. "You got it. Plus they were also paying Granz back for integrating the concert. He refused to have separate seating for white and blacks."

Harry spoke then. "Ah, ha. So that was the real reason for the raid. Revenge."

I said. "Jesus, the crap black musicians had to put up with. It's unbelievable."

Dee was warming up to the subject. "It wasn't only black musicians they went after. They arrested the Baroness what's her name, you know the rich woman from Europe who helped cats when they were down. 'Member, Charlie Parker was staying in her apartment when he died?"

"Yes, I heard about that. Didn't he write a song for her?"

"No, not him, Monk did. He called it 'Pannonica.' Well, this one time she was driving Monk and Charlie Rouse to Baltimore for a gig when the cops stopped them, probably 'cause they saw a white woman with two black men. Anyway, they searched them and the car. They found some strands of pot in the bottom of the Baroness's purse and took the three of them to the station." She paused.

"Jesus. She got off, I hope."

"No, she didn't. They dismissed the men, but arrested her. Imagine, arresting a Baroness? They sentenced her to three years, just for having strands, not even a joint. She fought it for two years, spending a fortune on lawyers, and finally got the case dismissed."

Dee took a sip of her drink. "And there was Anita O'Day. They went after her just as bad as Georgia."

Both Harry and I looked at her. I asked. "You mean the gal who sang with Gene Krupa and Stan Kenton? But she was white."

"Um, um. When it came to harassing jazz folks, the cops were color blind. Every time she had a gig anywhere, the Feds would alert that city's police department. So they'd go to her concerts, search her dressing rooms and hotel suites, usually without a warrant, hoping to catch her with some kind of shit. 'Course they finally did bust her."

I remembered another story. "And what about Gene Krupa? His assistant was arrested when he came out of Gene's room carrying a jacket. The narcs searched the kid and found a joint. The kid said Krupa had sent him to pick up the jacket. Well, Krupa was arrested and it was a big, big deal. They wanted to give him a long sentence. The upshot was the kid testified he'd been coached by the narcs to lie, and Krupa was freed."

Harry exclaimed. "Good grief. What about civil liberties? How the hell could they get away with that stuff?"

I said. "Well, how come we're putting terrorist suspects into prison without due process? And incarcerating illegal immigrants who've lived here peacefully for years? And searching people without probable cause. The beat goes on."

No one spoke. We'd depressed ourselves with our depiction of American injustice.

Dee turned to me and gave me a pointed look. "Okay, Casey, now do you think it's possible that Georgia Valentine was murdered?"

Chapter 5

IT WAS A week later. I paid the cab driver and trotted up the stairs to the entrance of my building, happy as hell to be home. As soon as the front door closed, Mrs. Wong appeared at her door, which was opposite the front entrance. She must have super hearing. She opened her door whenever I entered or left. "You home. Good. Here's mail."

She held out a paper bag, which I took, thanking her, and then retreated into her apartment. The bag was full. It was amazing how much mail I got in a week, even though I did most of my communicating via email.

Taking it upstairs, I went into my sanctum, threw my luggage on the floor and sighed. Home. Without even taking off my jacket, I checked my land line for messages, finding only a reminder for a dentist appointment, and opened my emails. I'd checked while I was away, so there were only ten or so new ones, mostly appeals for political donations or to buy products I didn't want or need.

I'd been in Los Angeles doing interviews for Barton-Lehman, which had a contract for vetting employees of a company one of their clients had taken over. Why these long-term workers had to be checked again was beyond me. It seemed a waste of time and effort, but who am I to question the hand that feeds me?

I was eager to get over to Dee's to hear some good music. I hadn't even phoned while I was gone, having been busy every day and not wanting to bother Dee at night when she was working. Dee and her club had been a part of my life for so long, not going over there was a serious deprivation, like not seeing the sun.

I took a quick shower, changed into my going-out clothes, a T-shirt and jeans, boots and leather jacket, and fast-walked over to the club, about eight blocks away. I savored the sights and smells of Chinatown and North Beach, thankful as always that I lived in such a cool neighborhood.

I smiled as I turned the corner and saw Dee's neon sign, but the smile quickly disappeared as I noticed it was dark. Something was wrong. I stepped up to the door and read the sign *CLOSED UNTIL FURTHER NOTICE.* What the hell? My stomach churned. Had something happened to Dee?

I stepped to a door a few feet from the club entrance, the entrance to Dee's upstairs apartment. It was very plain, painted a dark gray, designed to discourage people from entering. I pressed the buzzer on the security system and wanted for a response.

When I heard Dee's "Yes?" I breathed a sigh of relief. She was okay.

"It's me, Casey? What's wrong? Why is the club closed?"

Dee waited a moment before answering. "So you're back. You better come up."

The buzzer sounded and I stepped into the hall. A door on the right led to the club and a flight of stairs on the left went up to Dee's apartment. The stairs were covered with a bright red carpet, and a gold star was affixed to her apartment door, gifts from Barney, Dee's late husband and most devoted fan.

Dee was waiting for me at the top of the stairs, a somber expression on her face.

I climbed the stairs without speaking. Once we were ensconced in her living room, each with a drink, I asked her what had happened.

Dee was minus her usual feistiness, her mouth downturned and her eyes sad. "The health department closed me down, saying we weren't up to standard."

"What?" I exclaimed. "You who are so persnickety about cleanliness?"

She smiled briefly. "Yeah, me. After all these years of never a blemish on my record, not to mention Barney's before me, they said we didn't pass muster."

"But why? How?"

"They gave me some bullshit about poor sanitation. The water wasn't hot enough. Angelo didn't wash his hands thoroughly. A load of crap."

Angelo had been Dee's cook for many years and was used to Dee's ways, one of which was an insistence on cleanliness.

I frowned. "That's unbelievable. Was it a new inspector?"

She nodded. "Yeah, the motherfucker. He inspected everything. And he had this attitude."

I wondered if Dee had antagonized him. "Did you give him a bad time?"

"Hell, no. I left the kitchen so's I wouldn't. I was pissed, yes, but I didn't say a word. I let him do his thing. When I got the report, I was shocked out of my mind."

"What are you gonna do?"

"Well, I plan to do some upgrading, put in some stainless steel counters, modernize. I been wanting to do that anyway. But even though the kitchen is old, it's clean, goddammit." She'd gotten a little of her energy back.

"Then what?"

"Then I get another inspection and re-open."

"This will cost you some money."

She sighed. "I know. I have to use some of my savings, but I got no choice. Those bastards got me by the short hairs."

"Have you looked at the report?"

"Only the final assessment. My total points were below the requirement."

I had a thought. "Why don't I get the report so we can see exactly what his objections were?"

She brightened. "Can you do that?"

"Damn right. You have a right to see it. I'll see about getting it for you."

She actually smiled. "Okay, good. I feel better already. Now tell me what's happening with the Georgia Valentine case."

Chapter 6

I LOVED MANHATTAN. It's San Francisco times ten. More people, more buildings, and, if that's possible, more traffic. Take any ten people walking down a street and you'll see ten styles of dress, ten skin colors, and hear ten languages. To call New York City diverse is to make the understatement of the century.

I came into JFK last night. Freddy Clarke picked me up and brought me to the apartment of a musician friend who's on tour. I'd spent the previous week catching up on reports for my regular client, and two days ago the handwriting expert I'd hired called to tell me that the Georgia Valentine letter was authentic. After I reported this to Freddy, he lost no time in getting me an airline ticket, arranging a place to stay, and setting up interviews.

Investigating Georgia Valentine's death as a murder was a big deal, all right. It was the most important case I'd ever worked on. And I was excited. As well as nervous. I didn't want to mess up with so many people depending on me.

After Freddy dropped me off at the apartment, I looked around, then went to bed, having gotten up at four to make my seven o'clock flight. The apartment was fine, small, but it had a bathroom, a kitchen and a bed. What else does a person need? It was obviously a man's pad, could be a little neater, but, as the saying goes, the price was right.

As soon as I awoke, I got dressed and went out. The apartment was on 3rd Street between A and B streets in what's known as the East

Village. I turned left and walked along the block, hoping to find a good cup of coffee. The street was lined with commercial establishments, a flower stand, a pizza place, a bakery, a video rental store, and sundry restaurants, Chinese, Middle Eastern, Indian, Japanese, Italian, and a kosher Mom and Pop. And they were only a few of the eating places I saw in that one block. I'd guess there were five people within any ten foot square area of street, walking purposefully to god knows where.

I spotted a Starbucks and a feeling of familiarity enveloped me, like seeing a hot dog stand in the middle of a Moroccan bazaar. Later I'd try something different, but for now, I wanted the familiar. I ordered my usual mocha and took it to a comfy chair by the window, thinking about the day ahead.

Freddy had arranged for me to interview John Beasley, a good friend of his who had known and worked with Georgia Valentine and whose wife had been close to her. The name was familiar and, after looking him up on the Internet, I discovered he was one of the most respected tenor saxophone players in jazz.

I felt like that guy in the Woody Allen movie who time-traveled and ended up meeting Hemingway, Fitzgerald, Stein and other famous dead writers. But instead of going back to Paris in the Twenties, I was going back to New York during the heyday of jazz, the Fifties. And the people I was meeting were alive, not ghosts, thank heaven.

I was seeing John at one o'clock at the office of Regency Records, his long-time label. Since he had to come into the city to take care of some business, he suggested we meet there, to save me a trip to his home in Teaneck, New Jersey, seventeen miles from Manhattan. That was very kind of him, considering I had no clue how I'd get there.

It was enough of a challenge to get from my temporary apartment to the Regency office. With the help of a subway map, I'd got a rough idea of the route. The office was on 73rd Street in what they call the Upper East Side. I allowed an hour, just in case I got lost. I was looking forward to the meeting, although I had no idea what I'd say. I wasn't worried. The field of inquiry, fifty years of jazz history, was wide open.

From the apartment, I walked one block to the Second Avenue station, where I had to take the F line to 14th and transfer. Signs directed me to the appropriate platform, where I was overjoyed not to run into any rampaging teenagers or rats. I spent several minutes figuring out the ticket vending machine, and then several more inspecting the large subway map next to the machines. It was simplicity itself, the subway lines color-coded with large dots indicating stops. The New York subway system definitely had an undeserved bad rep. It was a snap.

After a few minutes of pacing next to the tracks and glancing at the large dark hole where the train would emerge, a red light flashed and the train roared into the station's open space, screeching to a halt in front of me and the other people waiting to board. Doors opened automatically and a horde of passengers poured out, and we all climbed in. Everyone seemed to be in a hurry. I imagined a subway didn't dally, so if you didn't enter promptly, you'd be left at the station.

Safely aboard, I took a spot next to the door, my right hand firmly gripping a steel bar. I didn't want to miss my stop, so I kept an eye on the map next to the door and mentally checked off each station as we passed it. When we arrived, I made sure to be the first one off. Then I went to another platform, where I caught the number two line. Mine was the third stop. I sighed with relief. I'd made it okay. My first New York subway ride wasn't as bad as I'd imagined.

The street was lined with brick townhouses, just like the ones you see in the movies, with small trees lining the sidewalks. As I walked, I thought about what Freddy told me about Beasley. He'd started out just as the Big Band era was winding down, spent some time studying music, and then joined one of the most popular bands in the country. Like so many other jazz musicians, he went to Europe in the late Sixties and, when he came back, he played with other orchestras and small groups. He'd performed with Georgia Valentine on many occasions, including European tours, and knew her quite well. And he'd also accompanied my friend, Dee Jefferson.

I got to 73<u>rd</u> and checking the numbers, turned left. The townhouses were butted up against each other, the front doors about ten steps up from the sidewalk. Once residences, they'd been converted into apartments or offices. At first I couldn't find the address and no wonder, it was one of those doors where you have to walk down several steps below street level, originally the entrance for tradesmen and servants.

Nothing on the door indicated it was the office of Regency Records. All it had was a brass plate displaying the numbered address. I pulled out my notes and checked. Yes, I had it right, so unless Freddy had made an error or I had, this was it.

I took a deep breath and knocked. No answer. I tried again. Nothing. I tried the handle and the door opened into a small office with a cluttered desk and a couple of worn leather chairs. One wall consisted of an overflowing bookcase and the other was covered with posters of all shapes and sizes, some yellowed with age. I stepped up closer and saw they were announcements of concerts and record albums produced by Regency Records. I was in the right place.

Chapter 7

I HEARD MALE voices behind a door leading to an interior office. I stepped closer and knocked before opening the door. Three men turned simultaneously to check me out. One man, a tall, white-haired African-American gentleman, said. "You must be Casey McKie."

"And you're John Beasley."

I smiled and held out my hand. We shook and he returned my smile, displaying a set of perfectly-formed teeth.

The other two men introduced themselves. I assumed they worked for Regency. They turned away and each took a seat at a desk, the only two in the small, windowless room.

John ushered me back to the outer office. "We can talk better out here."

He looked straight at me, his dark brown eyes intense. "Now what's this all about? Something about a letter from Georgia?"

I related the back story, about how Freddy got the letter from the late musician Bobby Walton's trunk, summarizing its contents. "Freddy and Dee think it may have a bearing on Georgia Valentine's death. They asked me to look into it."

"Ah, yes," he smiled slightly, "people have always said she didn't kill herself. They don't want to believe it."

I met his gaze. "Maybe she didn't."

"Maybe not. And this is what you've set out to prove?"

"Yes, one way or the other."

He sighed. "That's quite an undertaking, young lady, do you realize that?"

"Yes, sir, I do." Something about him made me want to address him formally. He had that kind of dignity.

He leaned forward. "And what if you find that she did in fact commit suicide?"

"Well, then. We'll know, won't we?"

He laughed. "I like you. Say, how's my girl Dee?"

"She's good. She's closed the club temporarily to upgrade the kitchen. But she's doing fine. The club is a success and she's singing great."

He sat back. "Good, glad to hear it. I always thought she was a helluva singer. I'll have to get out there one of these days."

"She'd love to see you."

He shifted in his chair. "How can I help you?"

I leaned forward again. "Well, you can answer this for me. Do you think it's possible that someone gave Georgia Valentine an overdose?"

He stared me in the eyes. "Yeah, sure. It's possible."

"Who do you think could have done it?"

He laughed again. "Now, that's the question, isn't it?"

"Can you make a guess?"

He looked off into space. After a few seconds, he said. "No, I sure can't."

"Do you think it could have been the Feds?"

His laugh was short and bitter. "God almighty. Wouldn't that be something? All's I know is that they kept records on all the big name jazz people. This journalist got all the public records and wrote about it." He paused to take a breath. "It started back in the Thirties with Cab Calloway and Duke Ellington. They kept track of where they went, where they performed, and who they knew. They were afraid they might be communists."

The idea was so ridiculous, I felt like laughing. But I remembered hearing about the McCarthy hearings in the Fifties when a power-mad senator made life miserable for artists and movie people by accusing them of betraying their country. Many of those falsely accused were blacklisted and couldn't get work for years.

"I've heard that, and Georgia was one of the ones they most wanted to catch. But she wasn't a communist, was she?"

He laughed. "Georgia, a communist? She probably didn't know what that was."

"So why were they after her?"

He raised his brow. "'Cause of drugs. And they did get her. She went to prison for a year. I suppose you heard that."

"Yes, that's when she got clean."

"And I heard she was doing okay after she got out."

I met his gaze. "That's why Freddy and Dee don't believe she injected herself. She was supposed to be off the stuff. That's what she said in her letter."

John frowned. "Did you know those bastards came to her hospital room and searched it while she was sick?"

"Yes, Freddy mentioned that."

John's eyes were dark with anger. "I wouldn't be surprised if they were so disappointed not to find any junk they gave it to her out of spite." He sat back, letting out his breath.

That was my theory, too. "Could that have happened?"

He shrugged. "Sure, why not? Those guys would intimidate anyone. They're in there with her, no one else around. They inject her, leave the fixings and let the nurse find her dead."

I mulled over that scenario. "It's an interesting theory. I'll have to check it out."

He smiled. "I would imagine that's the sort of thing you're good at."

"But I have to start somewhere. Do you know anyone who knew Georgia and who's still around?"

"Yeah, my wife. Bernice worshipped her and saw her a lot when she was in the hospital."

The interior door opened and one of the Regency men stepped through to where we were sitting.

"Excuse me. I forgot to offer you some coffee. I just made a fresh pot. Want some?"

We both answered in the affirmative. The man disappeared for a few moments while we sat silently, thinking over the scenario John had described. We didn't speak again until we had our coffee cups in hand.

John said. "Say, Casey, what are you doing tonight? There are some guys you should meet. They knew Georgia. They're at the Vanguard. My wife and I are going. We could meet you there."

I beamed. "That'd be great. I've always wanted to go to that club."

Dee always spoke of the Village Vanguard with reverence. It was the oldest jazz club in New York, having been started back in the 1930s. It was still going strong and hadn't changed owners since it was first established. After the founder died, his wife, who was quite a bit younger, took it over and was still running it. What other establishment has had the same owners for eighty years? If they'd sold it, it would probably have been remodeled and transformed into a hip hop club. Or a pizza parlor.

John said. "I didn't see much of Georgia at that time. I was working. But Bernice did. And so did these guys. They could help you out more than I can." He took a sip of coffee.

"Who are they?"

"The Moore brothers, Herman and Leroy. You know them?"

"I've heard Dee speak of them. Aren't there four brothers, all jazz players?"

"Yeah, and they're all great. But Willard and Marvin are gone, so it's just Herman and Leroy now. Piano and drums. They have a trio. With Roy Anderson on bass."

"Sounds terrific. About nine, then?"

"I'll call the owner, Lucille, and reserve you a seat at my table. Get there a little early. If you're a minute late, she'll give away your spot."

"I'll be there, looking forward to it."

Chapter 8

I LEFT JOHN at Regency. I had the impression he had more business to take care of. When I told him I'd be at the Vanguard at eight, an hour ahead of time, he smiled.

I had five hours to fill. Should I call Aaron? I hadn't told him about coming to New York. We hadn't talked for a few weeks, and I had the feeling his ardor was cooling. Mine, too, I guess, since it didn't bother me not to hear from him. And I hadn't called him either.

The truth was we had no future together, being geographically incompatible. He lived and worked in New York, and I, in San Francisco. Neither of us wanted to move. So that was that. Back to square one. I was thirty-six with no prospects of a partner. And of motherhood.

Even so, I should call him, out of simple courtesy. But part of me didn't want to. I didn't want to tell him about the case. It was a big deal for the jazz world, and I wasn't sure I could trust him, as the editor of a major jazz magazine, to keep quiet about it. If Georgia Valentine had been murdered, I'd have a better chance of catching her killer if he didn't know someone was after him. After fifty years, he'd probably lost all fear of being caught. If I could catch him off guard, it would make my job easier.

So, instead of calling Aaron, I decided to check out one of New York City's must-see sights, Lincoln Center. According to my map, it wasn't too far from the Regency Record office. All I had to do was walk down Broadway to Columbus. It was fairly warm and a walk would be nice.

Broadway was lined with smallish trees and huge buildings. I threaded through the ever-present pedestrians, all walking at a brisk pace. Was everyone in New York in a hurry? And was it crowded everywhere? I imagined so, given Manhattan, according to my guide book, had over eight million residents squeezed into twenty-two square miles. I was on Broadway, the famous street, but nary a sign of a theater. Where were they?

After walking several blocks, longer than I expected, I reached Lincoln Center. It was huge. Several very wide steps led up to a plaza, which was larger than the proverbial football field, a very big fountain in its center. Lining the square were some of the most famous music venues in the world, the Metropolitan Opera; Avery Fisher Hall, home of the New York Philharmonic; and the Rose Building, where the Lincoln Center Jazz Orchestra performed. The Rose was also home to the jazz venue, Dizzy's Coca Cola Club. Also at the center were The New York City Opera, the Juilliard School of Music, the New York Library and two theaters. Just the place for a culture vulture.

I could almost feel the ghostly vibes of Pavarotti, Callas, Beverly Sills, and Dizzy himself as I wandered around reading the playbills for tonight's events, a choice of two plays, a ballet, an opera, a jazz concert, and something called an intimate evening of song, featuring a well-known star of British musical theater.

I wished I had time to attend all of them, but that would have to wait until another day. I was on a mission, and, fortunately, that mission included a trip to the Village Vanguard.

I decided to find a place to eat rather than go back to the apartment, which was on the other side of town. I found a deli. It was unlike any deli I'd ever seen. It seemed to have everything, groceries, baked goods, the usual array of cheeses, meats, prepared salads, sandwiches, and condiments.

What intrigued me most was the homemade soup. I got a bowl of chicken noodle and a fresh roll from the bakery case and sat at one of the four tables at the back. I picked up someone's discarded newspaper, and ate my dinner while catching up on the events of the day, all of which were depressing.

The food was surprisingly good, the soup not loaded with sodium, and the roll, fresh. Now, if they served good coffee, I'd be in heaven. I gave it a try and found it okay. But that's all right. I have very high coffee standards. And the whole thing cost me less than ten bucks.

I didn't feel like going underground, so I hailed a cab and within minutes, one magically pulled up to the curb. After a few minutes of fast, weaving-thru-traffic driving, we pulled up to the dark red awning of the historic jazz club. The ride cost me thirteen bucks, not too bad. And I'd been told New York was horribly expensive. So far, I hadn't found that true. But, then, I hadn't been here that long.

Not too many people were around, only a group of Japanese, looking like they were waiting for the club to open. I went over to the dark red door, opened it to a flight of steep stairs, at the bottom of which a man stood behind a small podium. I went down and gave him my name. I held my breath to see if he'd admit me to what seemed more like a private than a public establishment.

I heard loud chattering behind me. The Japanese were on their way down. The man glanced at me, checked over the list, seemingly finding my name, since he crossed out something and nodded. I was in.

The room, a dark, windowless basement with lots of red accents, wasn't big, probably holding a hundred people max. Behind the stage at the far end of the triangular-shaped room hung a red velvet curtain. A row of small tables along the left and right walls stood in front of long red vinyl covered banquettes. The middle area was filled with small cocktail tables and wood chairs, crammed close together.

To the right was a bar with four red vinyl covered stools, set against a wall covered with an abstract red and yellow mural. The total effect was one of vintage intimacy, just what you'd expect of an historic jazz club.

I was early. Only a few people were at the bar. I sat at a table on the left hand side close to the stage. I craned my head around to check out the wall behind me. It was covered with a hodge-podge of framed photographs and drawings of jazz musicians. I recognized some of them, Miles Davis, Ella Fitzgerald, Georgia Valentine, Louis Armstrong, but the rest were unknown to me, there being more saxophone players than vocalists. With a little imagination, you could feel the vibes from the thousands of jazz riffs that had filled this room over the past eighty years.

After some animated conferring, the Japanese tourists settled in the middle of the room, taking up the first two rows. They spread out, leaving some of the chairs vacant. A stern-faced older woman, white-haired and dressed in black, came over and spoke to them. I couldn't hear what she said, but, as soon as she walked away, they regrouped, leaving no empty chairs. I guessed she was the owner I'd read about, known for her, shall we say, direct approach.

I sat there contentedly people-watching as the place filled up. John Beasley came in with an attractive black woman, spotted me and gestured. I smiled and waved them over. John introduced me to his wife, Bernice, who had apparently been visiting a friend while John was at Regency Records. We exchanged small talk for several minutes. Then she mentioned the subject that had brought us together.

"John tells me you're a private detective looking into the death of Georgia Valentine."

I flinched and looking around us, hoping no one had overheard her.

I leaned toward her and said softly. "Yes, but I'm trying to keep it as quiet as possible for the moment."

She drew her hand to her mouth, "Oh, I'm sorry." She lowered her voice to just above a whisper. "It's about time someone paid attention to her death. I never believed Georgie gave herself an overdose. Not after spending all that time getting clean in prison."

John smiled. "Bernice was a great friend of Georgia's. She was very upset when she died."

Bernice said. "I loved her. She was such a wonderful singer. And a sweet woman. And very funny. She was a darling."

I hadn't heard Georgia described in these terms, but then I hadn't spoken to any women. Men described her differently, usually emphasizing her physical attributes. Just then, the music began. I had been so involved chatting, I hadn't noticed the trio come onto the stage.

John leaned over and whispered, "The Moore Brothers, Herman on piano and Leroy on drums, Ray Anderson on bass."

I sat back and prepared to enjoy the music. It was what I called real jazz, when you recognized the melody and you couldn't help but move to the beat. I felt my right foot keeping time and Bernice was smiling and nodding her head to the rhythm. Every so often John would let out a quiet "Yeah."

The trio varied the set, doing ballads, up tempo tunes, and a couple of Latin numbers. I found it extremely enjoyable, even without a singer.

At the end of the first set, most of the audience left. The manager announced we could stay for the second set if we wished, as seats were available. John went up to talk to Herman and Leroy and then went back with them to the Green Room. Bernice stayed put and I understood I should also.

Chapter 9

BERNICE PUT HER hand on my arm. "Casey, don't forget about Maurice Leblanc."

I looked at her, puzzled. "Maurice Leblanc? Who's he?"

Her eyes were intense. "Georgie's husband." She thought a moment and added. "The one she was married to when she died."

I didn't remember that name from my research. Perhaps I'd skimmed over it. "What makes you say that?"

She made a face. "Because he was a real son of a bitch. I loved Georgie, but she picked the worst men."

"What was wrong with him?"

She sniffed. "What wasn't wrong with him? He only cared about one thing, Maurice. He used Georgie. She was making good money then, real good, and he took all of it. 'Course he bought her diamonds and furs, you know, but he also spent plenty on himself, fine clothes and a fancy car. And drugs. They spent a lot of money on drugs." She paused and took a sip of her drink. "Not too many people know this, but when she was arrested the first time, she was taking the rap for him."

I raised my eyes in surprise. "I hadn't heard that."

"No, she didn't tell many people. But she told me."

I leaned over the table towards her. "Tell me."

She took a deep breath. "Well, they were at the Jack London Hotel in San Francisco. She was performing at a club there. Maurice was in the audience, sitting with some of his pals. After the set when Georgie and Maurice were in their room, they heard a loud knocking on the door, the kind only the police can make. "Maurice handed Georgie a bag of dope and told her to flush it down the toilet. But the Feds got to her before she could get rid of it, and they arrested her. Maurice didn't say a word. He had a prior, see, and I guess they figured she'd get off light 'cause it was her first offense. So she went with them without protest. Luckily she had a good lawyer and got off."

"Jesus, that was risky. Why'd she do it?"

Bernice sighed. "'Cause that's how she was with men. Her other men weren't much better."

"But then she was arrested again, right?"

Bernice looked me directly in the eyes. "Yes, but it was suspicious. She was performing in New York. When she got to her dressing room after the show, the Feds were waiting for her. They searched everywhere and found a small packet of heroin. They handcuffed her and took her to the station. This time she got a year."

"Yeah, that's when she got clean, right?"

Bernice nodded. "Yes, after she got out, she was different, more mature. She vowed to stay off dope and to take better care of herself."

"You mean health-wise?"

"No, I mean take charge of her career. She'd put herself in the hands of men who were taking advantage of her, not only Maurice, but Morey Stein, too."

I'd heard the name. "You mean her manager?"

Bernice nodded. "Yes, you should ask John about Morey. He knew him."

"How did her new attitude affect Maurice?"

"Well, she told him she'd be in charge of her money from then on. She said he'd have to carry his own weight. In other words, get off his ass and get a job. And she threatened to divorce him."

"And how'd he take that?"

She pursed her lips. "What do you think? He didn't like it. Not one bit. Let's put it this way. Soon after she made this declaration, she died. And he got her money." Her eyes were fierce.

I didn't answer right away, letting this sink in. "So if I understand you correctly, you're saying that Maurice may have killed her."

She met my gaze. "Yes, honey, I sure am."

John came back to the table as the trio took their places for the second set. I noticed they did more up tempo numbers this time around and seemed to be taking more chances, deconstructing the melodies more radically. I usually found this kind of improvising annoying, but with these guys, it was different. I actually enjoyed it, but didn't know enough about music to know why.

When the set was over and people were leaving, John rose from his chair. "Come on, Bernice, I want Casey to meet Herman and Leroy."

He led us down the hallway to a room where the trio was relaxing. It wasn't your standard green room. It must have once been a kitchen, a fridge, a sink and dishwasher were still in place, and it obviously doubled as an office, for a cluttered desk stood against a wall covered with photographs of musicians, usually with an arm around a short, balding man I assumed was the club's founder. Next to the desk was a bank of shelves filled with cleaning supplies, paper towels and other paraphernalia.

A group of wooden chairs stood haphazardly in the center of the room. Herman and Leroy were occupying two of them, but stood as we entered. They greeted Bernice warmly, and John introduced me. Then he left to get us drinks, a whiskey highball for his wife and a white wine for me. Bernice made small talk until he returned.

After some discussion about mutual friends, John said to the Moore brothers. "Casey is investigating the death of Georgia Valentine. I hope you guys can help her out."

Herman said. "Sure, we'd like to if we could. We never believed she took that shit in the hospital. She was clean then. But, man, that was a long time ago. What can anyone do about it now?"

"Yeah," his brother echoed.

John looked at me.

I answered them. "Well, it's what you do in any case, cold or not. You gather evidence. It might be harder because of the passage of time, but it's not impossible. Cold cases are investigated all the time. People are still trying to figure out who killed President Kennedy."

Both men nodded. "What can we tell you?"

I said. "Well, to get right to the point, is there anyone who might have wanted Georgia Valentine dead?"

Herman emitted a short laugh. "That is getting right down to it." He glanced at his brother. "What do you think?"

Leroy took a swallow of his drink. "I can think of more than one."

This surprised me. I waited for him to elaborate.

Leroy sighed. "Her old man, for one. I heard she was gonna dump him. Without her supporting him, that lazy motherfucker might have had to go to work."

His brother said. "Yeah. He was a total prick."

Leroy continued. "And there was Morey. That cheap bastard cheated her. He'd charge so much for a gig and keep most of it for himself. He'd be sweet as pie to your face, but stab you in the back the next minute. But after she got out of prison, she was a lot smarter than when she went in. She wasn't gonna put up with that crap no more. And she told Morey so, too."

Herman said. "I wouldn't put it past Morey to put out a contract on her. He'd done it before to people who crossed him."

I stared at him. "Jesus. Are you kidding me?"

"I wish I was. Morey Stein was connected to the mob. They set him up in the business, so they had a piece of the action. That's why he screwed all his artists. He had to pay them back."

I said. "Georgia must have made Morey some good money. She was big time there for a while."

"Yeah, playing Carnegie Hall and those European tours, she made a lot of bread. 'Course if she needed money, Morey'd give it to her, but why wouldn't he? He was getting rich off her and his other artists."

"How could he get away with cheating people like that?"

Leroy listened to what we were saying, but let his brother do the talking, "You could if you were Morey Stein."

I persisted with my questions. "What do you mean?"

"If you're backed by gangsters who'd kill someone as soon as look at 'em, you can get away with anything."

"But didn't the police do anything?"

"Nah, the mob had the police in their pocket."

"Jesus."

"But, Morey got his eventually. He was arrested for fraud soon after Georgia died."

"And now?"

"He's gone."

"So who's running the agency?"

"Morey's partner, Al Rosen, took it over, and after he died, his son got it. But you don't hear much about it. I don't know what the hell they do, 'cause they're not doing much booking."

"And you really think Morey Stein could have had Georgia killed?"

"Sure. She was threatening to rat on him for cheating her. Even though she was a junkie, she was a big star and if she complained to the powers that be, they might have done something. That would have scared the shit outta Morey."

I sipped my wine. The conversation seemed to have come to an end. I couldn't think of anything else to ask. They'd told me about two possible suspects. That was enough to chew on for now.

Chapter 10

In LESS THAN twenty minutes after I left the Vanguard, my taxi pulled up at my apartment building. I thought it was kind of cool the entrance was simply a set of double doors painted dark blue. It had an intercom plate with the names of the tenants, but that was it. It was very secretive.

Once in the apartment, my spirits sank. It's one thing to stay in a hotel room, but another to stay in someone else's pad. In a hotel, you can spread your things around and make it seem like home, but in an occupied place, you can't. You live out of your suitcase. This was a studio and every inch of space was filled.

The solution was to be here as little as possible. Tomorrow I had an appointment with an archivist at the Josef Katz Jazz Collection, where I was hoping to get some questions answered.

I got ready for bed and crawled under the covers with a sigh. But I couldn't get to sleep. My thoughts kept going to the two men I'd heard about tonight. It looks like Georgia couldn't trust anyone, certainly not her husband or her manager, the two people who were supposed to be looking out for her. Not only were they exploiting her, either one of them could have killed her.

Christ. I was beginning to believe Georgia really had been murdered. Everyone said she was clean after she got out of prison. And she'd decided to rid herself of the destructive men in her life. That could have motivated one of them to get rid of her, just like she said in her letter. With that cheery thought, I fell asleep.

I awoke refreshed, with no residual jet lag. I took a shower, got dressed and left the apartment at ten. This time I'd avoid the familiar and look for some local place for breakfast. I walked down Third and in the second block spotted an Italian bakery cafe on the corner. It looked upscale, but it shouldn't cost me much more than what I usually paid for my grande mocha.

I went in and stood in line, with about four people ahead of me. I looked over the choice of pastries and saw that they had my favorite, chocolate croissants. I ordered one along with a large cappuccino and took them to my table. As I ate my continental breakfast, my thoughts reverted to the case.

Even if Georgia's husband or manager had murdered her, how the hell would I ever prove it? If someone went to her hospital room pretending to be a doctor and gave her an injection, there were only two ways to substantiate it, by a confession or an eyewitness account. It seemed impossible to get either.

I took a bite of my croissant and a sip of cappuccino and couldn't help but give out a soft "Yum." Like the song says, little things mean a lot.

What was I supposed to do, give up? I imagined Dee's reaction if she heard me say that, disgust and disappointment. I'm known as someone who persists in the face of long odds. I'd have to carry on and see where it takes me. Stirring up the pot is bound to cause something to rise to the surface. Even if it's gunk.

Energized by my self-administered pep talk, I left the café and headed toward the nearest subway station. The Josef Katz Jazz Collection was on West 21st. I took one line for four stops and, voilá, there I was, at my destination. I loved the subway.

The door had a small printed sign identifying it by name. Very unpretentious. I entered the door to a small lobby, which had a couple of hard-backed chairs against one wall and a pass-through type counter with a bell sitting on it. I punched the ringer, its strident noise penetrating the silence. I waited a few minutes for someone to appear, contemplating a second clarion call, when a door opened.

"Yes, may I help you?" The speaker was a very short woman with lively dark eyes and curly dark brown hair, dressed in slacks and sweater, wearing a friendly smile.

"Hi, I'm Casey McKie and I have an appointment with M.K. Lehman."

"I'm M.K."

It was clear that the initials were how people addressed her. I wonder what it stood for, Mary Kate? Martha Katherine? "Nice to meet you. So you're the archivist?"

She nodded. "One of them. I understand you have some questions."

"Yes, a number of them." M.K., who'd been standing in the doorway, turned and gestured for me to follow. She led me down a hallway past several closed doors, then opened one, waving me inside. Walking behind her, I thought she must be the shortest normal person I'd ever seen. She was less than five feet, so diminutive you wanted to scoop her up like a big doll and give her a hug.

The office consisted of a library-sized table with a chair on either side. The only other furnishings were framed photographs of the jazz icons, Miles Davis, Charlie Parker, Ella Fitzgerald, Louis Armstrong, Georgia Valentine and a couple of others.

M.K. opened the conversation. "Tell me about your project."

I smiled, "But first can you tell me about this place? What is it exactly?" Freddy had told me that it held Georgia Valentine's papers and was where Bobby Walton's letter could be authenticated. I didn't know what else they had here.

M.K. smiled. "Sure, Josef Katz was an immigrant from Poland who came to New York in the Twenties. He lived in the Village and went out to hear jazz just about every night. He started buying records, 78s and then LPs. As time went on, he got more serious about acquiring recordings. He bought other people's collections and memorabilia. Eventually his house was filled to the brim, all four floors. When he died, he left the house and the collection to the city. They took it, but didn't know what to do with it. Eventually, they decided to make it part of the New York Library system."

"And how did you get involved?"

"Me?" She raised her brow. "I used to come here often to pick up a record I wanted. I got to know Joe. We had a lot in common, both of us crazy collectors and Jewish. When the library opened his house to the public, I applied for a job as archivist and got it."

"It must be interesting." I murmured.

M.K. searched my face to see if I were being ironic, and, deciding that I wasn't, answered.

"It is for someone like me. I get to hear some rare stuff and also acquire recordings for my own collection."

"You collect jazz recordings also?"

"Oh, yes." The way she said it told me she was a collecting fanatic. "Now how can I help you?"

Chapter 11

I TOLD HER about the letter found in Bobby Walton' s trunk, his family giving it to the New York Jazz Society, Freddy finding it and calling Dee, and Dee calling me. M.K. kept nodding. She knew Bobby, Freddy, and Dee. She remembered the woman who asked for a sample of Georgia's handwriting. She even remembered I was the one who solved the murders of Max Greenfield and Jane Lee Patterson.

"So how can I help you?" She repeated.

"Well, I want to know more about Georgia Valentine. I've read about her on the Internet, but I need to know more."

"Such as?"

"Her death, first of all. I read she died of an overdose while she was in the hospital for some kind of infection. I need more details."

M.K. sighed. "Okay, I'll tell you all I know." She took a breath. "She was in the Metropolitan Hospital and died on May 17, 1963. She was found by a nurse at 3:30 am, who called the resident on duty, who called the cops. She was declared dead at 4:43. They found a needle and an empty packet on her night stand. They also found a wad of money, a thousand dollars, ten hundred-dollar bills, rolled up and rubber-band-ed, taped to her body.

"The autopsy showed that the influx of drugs was recent, and the only sign of heroin in her system. There was only one fresh needle mark on her, on her upper arm. No others."

She paused, her eyes on mine. I said. "So they determined the cause of death was a drug overdose."

"Yes, although, in reality, it was due to respiratory failure caused by a massive dose of the drug."

"Did anyone suspect foul play at the time?"

She held up her hands. "Hey, I'm just an archivist. I don't have theories."

I bet she did, but I didn't press it.

I sat there thinking about what she'd told me.

M.K. interrupted my thoughts. "Do you know about Georgia's father?"

"No, nothing. What can you tell me?"

Her glance shifted upward as she searched her memory. "Quincy Valentine. He was just a kid when his girlfriend, Della Stamps, got pregnant, sixteen. Of course, he wasn't prepared to marry her. Della continued to live with her mother, who worked as a house cleaner, and Quincy continued to live the life of a single young black man." She sighed. "Who knows how many other young women he impregnated? Well, eventually, Quincy became a musician, played guitar. And he was pretty good, too. He worked with some well-known groups."

"Where is he now?"

"He died in 1964 in Chicago, of cirrhosis, age 64."

This woman must have a photographic memory as well as a prodigious interest in jazz history.

"What about the mother, Della?"

M.K. met my gaze. "She also outlived her daughter. She married and lived with her husband in New York until she died in 1972 of natural causes."

I glanced down at my notebook. "One more thing, did Georgia leave any money?"

"No, but she may have been due royalties. Many of these artists make more money dead than alive."

Jesus. How morbid. "Do you happen to know who her drug suppliers were?"

She laughed again. "No, never had an interest in that. But," she leaned toward me, "I can tell you who would know."

"Yes?"

"Dan Brennan."

"Who's he?"

"He's a jazz critic and writer. He wrote a book on jazz and drugs. It's called *Jazz, Pot, Smack and Crack.* It's considered the definitive work on the subject. You should talk to him."

"Where can I find him?"

"I know he lives in Manhattan somewhere. I can give you his number. Also you could reach him through *JazzBeat.* He writes a regular column for them."

Oh, oh, that zapped my nervous system. That was Aaron's magazine. Now I have a problem. Here I am in New York without having contacted him. I can't very well call one of his writers without calling him first.

But I didn't tell M.K. I knew the magazine's editor. "Good. I'll definitely get in touch. By the way, what happened to Maurice Le-Blanc?"

"He's actually still around. 'Course he's pretty old. I heard he lives at the Harlem Assisted Living Center. I don't have the number, though, but you can find it in the book."

She leaned back in her chair, taking a deep breath.

I got the hint. The interview was over. She'd given me lots of information and was probably tired from talking so much. I rose, as did she, and we walked back out to the lobby. I thanked her, bending slightly to shake her hand. She may be small in stature, but she had a monolithic memory.

Chapter 12

NOW WHAT? I had no other interviews scheduled although I had more people to see, Dan Brennan, for example.

But I had to call Aaron first. Brennan would be certain to mention he talked to me. If Aaron finds out about the investigation from someone else, he's more likely to publish the story. But if I ask him to hold off until I've finished, he would do it. I think.

Besides, I was lonely. I didn't realize how important Dee and Harry were in my life. I never felt lonely at home, even though I lived by myself. It was because I spent so much time at Dee's, which was basically my second home.

I spotted a Starbucks, there seemed to be one on every block, and went in to get a cappuccino and a comfy chair. Once I had both, I pulled out my cell phone and put in Aaron's number. I got a recording, so I left a message telling him I was in town and would like to see him. That would give him time to sort out a response.

I took a sip of cappuccino, sighing with pleasure. I really wasn't sure how Aaron felt about our relationship. Ever since we had that tiff over Dee's article, a frost had set in. Even though the problem was resolved, Aaron ran the article with only a few edits, our friendship hadn't been the same since.

It's interesting how people don't want to accept that Georgia committed suicide. It reminded me of what Dee said. Georgia Valentine was a heroine for black women. Men, too, I imagine. She was born into the toughest conditions, yet rose to the top of her profession. People didn't want to believe she took the easy way out. I don't like to hear negative comments about my heroes either and certainly wouldn't want to hear they committed suicide.

Georgia Valentine had a complicated life, filled with shady companions, several lovers and husbands, most of whom were less than model citizens, a manager with mob connections, and a horde of people who leeched off her, from drug pushers to family members. Some of them would do anything for money, and Georgia, after she became successful, was earning a lot of bread. In other words, a lot of people would benefit from her death.

My phone rang. It was Aaron. "Hey, what are you doing in New York?"

I explained, with just a touch of deception, that it was a last minute thing. Someone had hired me to do some research.

"Really? What kind of research?"

"It's a long story. I'll tell you when I see you." Of course, I really didn't know if I *would* see him.

"When did you get in?"

'Yesterday. I went to the Village Vanguard last night with my client." That was a bit of a stretch, but it would explain why I hadn't called him right away.

"Oh, you saw the Moore Brothers. How'd you like them?"

"Very much. I like their style of jazz."

"Yeah, it's very traditional. Right up your alley."

He was right. I much preferred the older jazz styles to the mishmash of what passes for jazz today.

"Yeah, it's the kind of jazz I like."

He blurted out. "What are you doing tonight?"

"No plans. Got something in mind?"

"Well, I'm going to hear a new group at the Jazz Standard. Want to go? But I must warn you, they're nothing like the Moore brothers."

I didn't think I needed a warning. I wasn't that close-minded, but I kept quiet. "That'd be great. Meet you there?"

Like a lot of New Yorkers, Aaron didn't have a car. He claimed it was cheaper and faster to use public transportation. It made very good sense. I've often thought of getting rid of my car, except San Francisco didn't have a city-wide subway system.

"Yeah, let's eat there. The food is pretty good. Can you make it at seven? Where are you staying?"

I explained I was using someone's apartment in the East Village and was fine with taking the subway.

Now that I'd told Aaron I was in town, I felt okay about calling Dan Brennan. I fished out the number M.K. had given me from my bag and called. I got a recording and left a message asking if we could meet tomorrow, explaining who I was and what I was doing.

The Jazz Standard was on East 27th, another easy trip on the subway. I'd left the apartment at six and arrived early. The entrance had two doors, one going up on the left to a restaurant, which seemed to specialize in barbecue, and one on the right leading to a set of stairs. The Jazz Standard, like the Village Vanguard was in the basement. Maybe all New York jazz clubs were underground. I went down the stairs, told the host I was meeting someone for dinner.

The bar was on the left, on a raised area with about ten tables, a railing separating it from the dining area, which was several feet lower. To the right was another seating area at the same level as the bar, also with a railing. The stage was farthest from the bar. Though it was separated into three sections, the place had an intimate feel, seating maybe a hundred and fifty.

I slid onto a stool, ordered a white wine, and picked up a schedule. I read a blurb about tonight's group, who went by the name *Special Fources*. They consisted of keyboard, drums, electric bass and horns. They were described as "metal drenched," "avant garde," and using "cross-genre stylizing." Their music was "jazz-based improvisation

50

with a bizarre equilibrium with loud and oscillating death-metal type grooves."

Huh? I didn't know what the hell they were talking about. But the use of the word "metal" raised a red flag. I had a sinking feeling I would have to spend the evening pretending to like music I couldn't stand. I sipped my wine and wondered how good an actress I was.

"Hey, Casey. Great to see you."

Aaron had come up behind me and planted a kiss on my cheek, taking the stool next to me. He looked cool and casual, his hair close-cropped, wearing a red turtle-neck sweater, jeans, a black leather jacket, and one of those small-brimmed fedora hats, very trendy.

"I was reading about tonight's group. Sounds intriguing," I lied.

"Oh? Don't know anything about 'em. I try to go see the new artists, part of the job."

"Sounds like a good gig."

He made a face. "Well, it's not as great as it sounds. Sometimes I don't feel like going out. And I don't always like the music I hear." He turned to face me. "It's good to see you. Tell me about your project."

I looked around. Too many people were within earshot. "Can we move to a table? I don't want anyone to hear."

Aaron raised his brow, then rose from the stool and gestured to the hostess, who led us to a table on the right.

As soon as we were settled, I answered his question. "I've been hired to investigate the death of Georgia Valentine, but I don't want people to know just yet."

Aaron's eyes widened. "What? She died of an overdose over fifty years ago. Everyone knows that. What's to investigate?"

Here we go again. Everyone reacts the same way. "Well, my clients think she may have been murdered."

"Holy shit."

I explained about the letter. Aaron listened intently, his gaze riveted on me. He didn't speak until I'd finished my narrative. "I'll be damned. But the letter doesn't say someone was out to murder her."

"No, but everyone I've spoken to so far tells me they wouldn't be surprised if someone did. It seems several people had a motive."

I had the impression he didn't know that much about Georgia's life, so I filled him in. I was surprised at how much I'd learned in such a short time.

The waiter came over and we ordered the specialty of the house, barbecue ribs, which goes with jazz like beans with rice. Aaron ordered a bottle of red wine.

As soon as the waiter left our table, Aaron asked. "Okay, let's say someone did murder her. How would you prove it?"

That was the big question, all right. "First, I have to find out who did it. If I find that out, then I have to figure out how they did it. And why."

"Jesus Christ, is that all?" His sarcasm was obvious.

I smiled. "Yeah, it's a challenge."

"You can say that again."

The ribs and wine arrived, and the music started. So we spent the evening eating, drinking and trying to see if we liked *Special Fources.* Talking about it helped me avoid thinking how much I disliked them. It seemed to me jazz was losing the elements that defined it in the first place, rhythm, feeling and spontaneity.

We shared a taxi home, with Aaron getting out first. He didn't say a word about my coming in. I was relieved I didn't have to use the excuse I'd prepared. He simply gave me a kiss on the cheek, saying "I'll call you." The typical brush off. I was both grateful and insulted.

Chapter 13

It was a gorgeous day, sunny and mild. After Dan Brennan learned I hadn't seen Central Park yet, he suggested we meet at the Boathouse Café and to enter the park at 72nd and Fifth.

After the bustle of the streets, the cafe seemed like another world. If you ignored the skyscrapers, it looked like the countryside. The restaurant had an outside deck overlooking a lake, where ducks and swans dotted the blue water and an occasional rowboat or gondola floated by.

I took a table outside and ordered a white wine. I sat there, perfectly relaxed, gazing at the tranquil scene while I waited for Brennan. I hoped he'd answer why the narcs targeted Georgia and what really happened the night she died. I didn't know if Brennan had the answers. Maybe I was expecting too much.

I watched a man and his son maneuver a mini sail boat across the lake, expressing their triumph with a high five. Out of the corner of my eye, I noticed an older man standing near the restaurant entrance, glancing about. Assuming it was Brennan. I stood and waved, hoping my hunch was correct.

He was about sixty, of average height, slim, wearing khaki slacks and a lightweight, blue athletic jacket. He had glasses and a scraggly beard. As he approached me, he smiled, and his appearance changed from non-descript to intriguing.

"Casey?"

I stood and we shook hands. He sat in the chair opposite me. "Nice spot, isn't it? One of my favorites hangs."

"Yeah, anything next to water is good."

I waved the waiter over and said to Brennan. "What would you like?"

"Just coffee for me, thanks."

"Nothing else? It's on me."

"No, thanks, coffee will be fine."

Once he was served, we took a good look at each other.

Brennan spoke first. "So you're a friend of Aaron's. He told me to treat you right or else he'd bust my ass." He said this with a smile.

"Funny, he told me the same thing."

He laughed. "So you're a private eye, huh? What happened to the tough guys in trench coats and hats pulled down over their eyes? Now we have -" He looked me up and down.

"Soccer moms?" I finished his sentence for him.

He laughed. "Yeah, you do look something like that. A nice woman who hasn't a violent bone in her body."

I smiled. "Well, I prefer to solve my cases without using violence, so you're not too far off."

"Kids?"

"Not yet. One day." I'd better take control of this conversation before it turned into an interview.

"I'd like to ask you a few questions, if I may."

The waiter brought the coffee and Brennan immediately picked up his cup. "Is this some kind of gimmick? You working on a book deal?"

I laughed. "No, I'm investigating Georgia Valentine's death because someone is paying me to do it. It's my job."

"Good answer." He gave me an intense look. "But I bet you don't take on jobs you don't like or can't do."

He was right there. "No, I don't. I like to win."

I could see the tension leave his body. I think I'd passed some kind of test.

He said. "I don't think I can help you. I don't know diddly-squat about Georgia Valentine's death. All I know is she was a junkie."

"Yeah, but someone recently found a letter she wrote just before she died saying she was clean and swearing she'd stay that way."

He pressed his lips together in a thin line. "They all say that."

"But she also said she was afraid someone was out to get her."

He grunted. "Sheer paranoia."

"But maybe not. Most of the people I've talked to think it's possible someone murdered her."

He didn't speak, resting his gaze on me for a few moments. "What do you hope to get out of this, besides your fee?"

He sounded cynical, but I thought his questions were coming from real curiosity, so I gave him an honest answer. "I could probably make the same amount working for my regular clients doing deep background checks. But I like a challenge. And besides I don't like the idea of someone getting away with murder. I don't care how long ago it was."

He said nothing, just looked at me appraisingly.

I leaned toward him. "But the most important reason is this. Georgia Valentine was a huge influence on a lot of people, singers, mainly, and they don't like the idea that she killed herself for whatever reason. They want her to be triumphant. If I can restore that legacy for her, I'd be very happy."

He gave me a high five. "All right. I'm convinced. Not that she was murdered," he paused, "but that you're sincere. So how can I help?"

I leaned back, taking a deep breath. "Okay, tell me this. Why did the narcs pick on her? From what I heard, they harassed her almost to the point of persecution. Was it because she was a woman? Black? Or both?"

Brennan smiled. "You know I wrote a book on the subject of jazz and drugs."

I nodded. "I know. That's why I wanted to talk to you."

His lips formed a slight smile. "Maybe you should read it." He took a sip of coffee. "But to save you the time, I'll give you a synopsis."

He took a deep breath. "It all started with a guy named Frederick Oblenger. He was made head of the Federal Narcotics Agency in 1931. He was obsessed, just like J. Edgar Hoover was at the FBI. His goal was to rid the country of drugs and drug users, mainly marijuana. That was before heroin and cocaine came into vogue.

"Pot wasn't used much in the early days. It came to the US through Latinos and blacks. Jazz musicians got it from them and used it to relax. Some cats thought it made them play better, but that was crap. Anyway, this fanatic Oblenger thought marijuana would fry your brain and make you go insane. Literally."

Brennan took another sip of coffee and continued. "Oblenger was instrumental in making pot illegal. He went to great lengths spreading the word on the 'evil weed.' He released stories about horrible crimes committed by men supposedly under its influence. He cultivated powerful legislators and the big drug companies. He was in charge of legal distribution, too, so the pharmaceutical companies sucked up to him. In fact, I heard a very powerful senator was in Oblenger's pocket because he kept him supplied with opium."

He paused to catch my reaction to this statement. I didn't disappoint.

"Have you seen 'Reefer Insanity?' Oblenger produced it as an educational film."

I nodded and smiled. "Yes, I've seen it. It's hilarious."

"Well, he didn't mean it to be funny. He was deadly serious. It was supposed to scare the shit out of teenagers, so they'd never use the stuff."

I smiled. "It didn't work, did it?"

"Hell, no, the kids discovered what Oblenger said about pot was bullshit, and so did a lot of other people. Scientists testified before Congress that Oblenger was wrong. Marijuana wasn't addictive and didn't incite users to violence. Doctors said addiction was a health issue, not a crime, and addicts should be treated not imprisoned. But Oblenger had instilled such fear in the populace that Congress was afraid to contradict him. It's like today when they vilify Al Gore and refute the science about global warming."

"But Oblenger and his boys went after Georgia for heroin, didn't they?"

"Yeah, if they thought marijuana was bad, heroin was evil incarnate. The problem was jazz geniuses like Charlie Parker used heroin, so other musicians figured if they used it, they'd be geniuses, too." He gave out a bitter laugh. "But it doesn't work that way. So the narcs went after jazz artists for smack as well as pot. They used any means to make a bust, the hell with civil rights."

"I heard they used illegal searches and entrapment."

"Yeah, that and making deals with informants. They'd let a junkie go if he'd rat on his musician friends."

"Jesus. But what I don't understand is why they picked on jazz musicians."

He shrugged. "In those days, jazz musicians were considered scum. They didn't have the prestige they do today. Maybe because most of them were black, I don't know. Jazz had no clout. People thought it was crazy music played by drugged out scumbags."

"I still don't get it. Jazz musicians weren't gangsters or murderers."

He shrugged his shoulders. "I think the narcs were on a power trip. They were like big game hunters. The bigger the name, the greater the trophy. Movie stars, jazz musicians, they were the prey. Oblenger loved it when his agents busted celebrities. That got him more publicity and helped him stay in the job."

"How long was he in power?"

Brennan frowned. "Would you believe thirty years? He survived the liberal Franklin Roosevelt administration and lasted until Kennedy."

"So did JFK get rid of him?"

"Not right away. As soon as Oblenger heard they wanted to re-place him, he started ordering raids to show the public and the press what an important job he was doing. It worked for a while, but eventually Bobby Kennedy fired him." He took a sip of coffee. "In fact, Georgia Valentine played a part in that regard."

That comment got my attention. "How?"

"Well, someone reported to the narcs she was using drugs in her hospital room, which was ridiculous because she was hooked up to an IV as well as monitors and couldn't move very easily. They searched her room, and the press made a big deal out of it. Her fans were outraged and let people know it. Well-known musicians and movie stars protested. People picketed the hospital. They wouldn't let up. So the Kennedy boys promised to look into the matter. But after she died of a drug overdose, the whole thing died down. Oblenger stayed in power a few more years, until Bobby finally got rid of him, mainly because he was interfering with his own vendetta against the mob. He said it was the job of the Justice department to investigate gangsters, not the Federal Narcotics Agency."

"But people are still being arrested for having pot. And prisons are bursting with people arrested on drug charges."

Brennan sighed. "Yeah, it's crazy. But let someone propose making drugs legal. That's about as unpopular, and as sensible, as outlawing assault weapons. So we have to thank Frederick Oblenger for starting the so-called 'war on drugs.' That's his legacy."

"Jesus. He was probably proud of it, too."

"Yeah, he was."

We chatted some more about jazz, how it's changing for the worse, and parted, with Brennan saying I could call him any time.

Chapter 14

I WAS WALKING to the subway station, on my way back to the apartment, when my phone rang. It was John Beasley. After some chit-chat, he got to the reason for his call.

"Bernice and I were talking. We really believe in what you're doing and want to help. Can we take you to dinner tonight?"

I wasn't looking forward to an evening alone in that tiny apartment, so I jumped at the chance to go out. Besides, I welcomed their help. Though I protested, they insisted on picking me up, saying they were taking me to a favorite restaurant in Little Italy, not too far from me.

The restaurant was called Dante's, which John and Bernice had been patronizing forever. The interior was standard Italian, checkered tablecloths and signed photos of celebrities on the walls. The waiters had the bored look of people who'd worked in one place too long. We were seated right away at a corner table, where a young man promptly brought us water.

Bernice made some menu suggestions, all of which involved tomato sauce, the house specialty.

"But don't order it hot. It'll burn your mouth out," warned John.

Our orders placed and drinks served, whiskey highballs for them and a white wine for me, we started talking about Georgia.

Bernice, who was looking elegant in a black cocktail dress and silver jewelry, said. "I think you should look at Maurice." She'd mentioned him before, but hadn't told me all that much.

"Yes?" I leaned forward, giving her my full attention.

She took a sip of her drink, then began. "First of all, he was a pimp, a real one. He had a string of women. 'Course, after he hooked up with Georgie, he didn't need them anymore. He sponged off her." She shook her head. "Why she married him, I'll never know. She gravitated toward men like him, no good bastards. He wasn't the first."

John spoke up. "Yeah, remember Herman Walker? He was a slick son of a bitch."

Bernice nodded. "That's what I mean. She always went for the same kinda guy, good looking but no good. Anyway, Maurice took drugs, too. He bought the stuff for her, and probably took a cut." She said this with bitterness.

She continued. "And he hit her. There were times when she had black eyes and bruises on her arms. And now she's -" Her voice cracked and tears formed in her eyes. John handed her his handkerchief.

Jesus. I hated to hear crap like this. "Did he hit her when she told him she wasn't gonna support him anymore?"

Bernice answered. "It wouldn't surprise me, but he wasn't living with her then. You know, he had another family in California, a woman with his two kids. And guess who supported them?" She paused for effect. "Georgie. She let him handle her money and never questioned him."

"Jesus, he sounds like a real jerk." I said. "Bernice, did you visit Georgia in the hospital?"

Bernice said. "Yeah, but by myself. John was working."

"How sick was she?"

"She was real sick, emaciated like. She was a big girl, but she was skin and bones. Lots of people came to see her. Maurice, of course, was always there. As soon as he heard she was in the hospital, he showed up. Probably staking out his territory in case, you know."

"But wasn't she trying to be more independent?"

Bernice made a face. "Yeah, she wanted to divorce him. But she was too sick then to argue. He was domineering and aggressive. Always playing the big shot. When he'd never done anything in his life but leech off women."

"What happened to him after, after she -" I trailed off.

"After she passed?" Bernice had regained her composure, the anger back in her voice.

"Yes."

"Well, since they were still married, I suppose he got everything."

"Everything? Did she have a lot of money then?"

John answered, shaking his head. "I doubt it. She hadn't been working much. When they'd arrested her, they took away her cabaret card, so she couldn't work in New York."

I'd heard something about this card, but didn't know exactly what it was. My ignorance must have shown, 'cause John quickly explained.

"A cabaret card was issued by the NYPD to anyone working in New York clubs, from dishwashers to entertainers. If you had an arrest record, you couldn't get one, and if you got busted, you lost it. And without a card, you couldn't work in New York. For a jazz artist, that was a death sentence."

"Jesus. That's cold. Could you get it back?"

"I heard some cats bought them back, but it cost a fortune. It was just another way for cops to control jazz folks."

"So Georgia didn't have that much to leave."

"Nah, but she was getting royalties from her records, the later ones, anyway."

I looked hard at Bernice. "So then Maurice did have a motive to murder Georgia."

She met my gaze. "He sure as hell did, and I wouldn't put it past him."

The waiter brought our food along with a basket of sour dough and we dug in, not speaking except to exclaim how good the food was. And they were right, the sauce was out of this world.

We ordered coffee. It was John's turn to speak. He leaned his elbows on the table, holding his hands together under his chin.

"Maurice was a no good rat, but Morey Stein wasn't much better. Before he became a booking agent, he was with the mob, the Valente outfit. I don't know what he did, but I know he was connected to them. And they set him up in business."

"Why?"

"They needed legit businesses for handling their money."

"You mean laundering?"

He nodded. "Yes."

"Jesus. Did they have a hand in operating the business?"

He shrugged. "You'd never see them in the office, but they were involved. Morey had to report to them. And, I know they interfered when Morey got into trouble."

"What do you mean?"

John paused. "Let me think a minute." He took a sip of coffee. "One time Morey had an offer for Hughie Johnson to tour Europe for a lot of bread. Hughie was Morey's biggest artist and commanded huge fees. Well, this club had already booked him for the same date as the tour and wouldn't let him out of the contract. After the club owner met with a slight accident," John rolled his eyes, "he changed his mind. And Hughie went to Europe."

I'd heard of Hughie Johnson. He was the best known trumpet player in jazz at the time, and probably still was. "Jesus, that sounds like the mob. But Georgia was one of Morey's most popular artists. He wouldn't want to get rid of her, would he?"

John gave me a fierce look. "He might. She said she was gonna blow the whistle on him."

My stomach lurched. Now this sounded like a real motive. "What do you mean?"

John cleared his throat. "Well, while she was in prison, she had a lot of time to think, and she figured out Morey was cheating her. I think someone must have clued her in. He was charging high fees for her, but taking way more than his twenty percent. And he had been doing it for a long time."

Bernice, who had been sitting there listening, said, "Yeah, she told me she was gonna hire a lawyer and sue his ass for what he owed her. And it was in the thousands."

Jesus, this put a whole new light on things. "So Morey could have sicced the mob on her."

Bernice sneered. "And that motherfucker would have done it, too."

Chapter 15

THE PHONE WOKE me. It was a little after nine. I checked the caller ID. It was Freddy Clarke, my client.

After the usual pleasantries, he said. "I need to talk to you about how it's going. I gotta give a report to the Society."

"Sure, how do you want to do it, by phone or in person?"

"Face to face, that's the only way I can talk. Let's meet half way, okay? In Harlem. There's a great soul food joint there called Sylvia's. You like soul food?"

"Sure, I like any food that tastes good."

"Well, you'll love Sylvia's then. Say today at noon?"

"Okay. I'm used to the subway by now. No problem."

After I showered and got dressed. I walked over to Starbucks. In anticipation of a big lunch, I didn't order a croissant and congratulated myself on my self-discipline.

I checked my emails, caught up on the news and left the cafe at eleven, giving myself more than enough time. I hated to be late.

You couldn't miss Sylvia's. It was on Lenox Avenue and had a huge sign, purple with neon lights. I sat at one of the tables in the outside patio to wait for Freddy. A waitress brought me a glass of what looked like iced tea and a basket of corn bread, which was one of my favorite foods.

I munched on the bread and thought about what I was gonna tell Freddy. Not much, just a corroboration of our suspicions that some people did have motive and opportunity to murder Georgia Valentine. I hope he didn't expect more. I'd only been on the case a few days.

I was facing away from the subway station, so I didn't see Freddy approaching. I heard his deep, gravelly voice before I saw him.

"Hey, Casey, you look like you're enjoying that corn bread," he said with a chuckle. "Tasty, isn't it?"

I smiled and stood. "Yeah, if the rest of the food is as good as this, I'll be in hog heaven."

"Well, then, you're on your way to the Promised Land, girl." We walked to the entrance, but before we got there, my waitress opened the door for us. I got the impression good service was part of the Sylvia's experience.

The interior was typical of a place with a history. Covering the walls were signed photos of celebrities with an arm around a woman who had to be Sylvia. The place was divided into different spaces, a lounge to the right and another dining room to the left. It wasn't crowded, so the waitress led us to a table in front. It was set like you'd see at someone's house, the dishes and utensils kind of mismatched, very homey.

The waitress brought menus, a pitcher of iced tea and a basket of corn bread. Freddy took a bite of corn bread. "Hmm. Love this stuff." He gestured toward the menu. "Casey, do you know about soul food? You prob'ly ate it with Dee."

"No, I haven't. Dee isn't really into soul food. She likes her steaks." Dee came from Detroit, not the South.

"Okay, let me make some suggestions, fried chicken, collard greens and mac cheese. That'll give you a good idea of what it's about."

I nodded. "Mac cheese. I guess that's macaroni and cheese, right?"

"Yeah, it's one of black folks' favorite dishes. It's real good here."

To me, macaroni and cheese came in cans and was something you gave kids. Homemade mac and cheese would be a new culinary experience for me.

I had another piece of corn bread and enjoyed it thoroughly.

Freddy said. "I'm asking for a report so's I can tell the Society we're making progress. I don't want this to worry you, but some of them are skeptical about what we're doin'. They think it's a waste of money."

I felt the heat rise to my face. I didn't like to think people were unhappy with my work. "Well, remember I didn't promise I would find the murderer. All I can do is provide possibility and probability that a murder happened. Proof will be hard to come by. I'll do my best, but I can't guarantee anything."

He spread out his arms, "I know. I know. That's all I expect. But I have to give 'em something. Don't you worry. They got nothing else to do but gripe. I have great faith in you."

I relaxed a little. "Okay, good." I took a sip of iced tea. "This is what I discovered so far. There's no question Georgia was targeted by the narcs. The head of the FNA hated jazz artists and the bigger they were, the more he tried to bust them. A team of agents searched her hospital room a few days before she died but didn't find anything. They could have been so pissed, they went back and gave her an overdose. That's kind of a far out theory, but then killing someone is not your usual behavior."

Freddy listened with rapt attention, nodding.

I took another sip of tea and continued. "Maurice, her husband, was by all accounts a real lowlife. He leeched off her and skimmed off the money she paid him to get drugs. When she was released from prison, she threatened to cut him off and even get a divorce. This could have scared him enough to get rid of her. He was at the hospital often, so he had ample opportunity."

Freddy frowned. "That low-down son of a bitch. I wouldn't be surprised if he done it."

"And then there's Morey."

Freddy looked at me sharply. "Morey?"

"Yeah, Morey. I found out the mob set him up in business and basically oversaw all his dealings. And he was not always on the up and up. He took money from his artists' fees, above and beyond his commission. Especially from Georgia. She was making a ton of money. She trusted him and didn't pay that much attention to business."

I paused to take a breath. Freddy seemed to be transfixed on what I was saying.

I went on. "So when Georgia asked him for an accounting, he got nervous. He may have been so nervous, he asked his mob pals to take her for a ride, as they say in the movies."

Freddy looked aghast. "Goddamn. Morey?" He repeated.

"Yes, Morey. One of the mob goons could have sneaked into her room and offed her." I was warming up to my story.

"Morey? I can't believe it."

The waitress appeared with our food. It was steaming and my mouth actually watered. We dug in and didn't talk, except to exclaim how good everything tasted.

After we finished eating and I got through raving about soul food, we ordered coffee. Freddy resumed his questioning. "So what do we do now?"

I looked him in the eye. "I have to get evidence."

"So you really think it could be murder?"

"I can't be certain, not without evidence. But I have very strong suspicions it was. We have three parties who could have done it, so homicide is not that far-fetched. I think you can tell that to your Society."

When I got back to the apartment, I felt like staying in. I suppose the place was feeling more like home. Besides, after that huge lunch, I couldn't eat a thing. I stopped in at the video store next door, picked up a couple of movies, and spent the evening watching romantic comedies. It was relaxing.

In the middle of a scene with Tom Hanks and Meg Ryan, my phone rang. It was Aaron. He said he was free the next day and would go with me anywhere I wanted, the Empire State Building, the Statue of Liberty, Coney Island, wherever.

Joan Merrill

I told him I wanted to buy a knock-off purse for Dee. He laughed. "Well, I know where to go for that. My mother buys them all the time."

We agreed to meet at the Canal Street/Chinatown subway station about noon.

Chapter 16

THE NEXT MORNING, I did my usual routine, taking my laptop to Starbucks and checking my emails. No word from Barton-Lehman, thank god. I'd finished a big job for them before I left, so they probably wouldn't need anything for a while.

When I got on the subway at eleven, I was so comfortable traveling underground, I allowed myself to think instead of checking the map every second. It was nice of Aaron to offer to spend the day with me, but I hope he wasn't imagining our relationship had a future.

When I'd met him on the cruise, I told him I was ready to settle down and have a family. He said he wanted the same things, so that's why I started seeing him. But so far we'd only spent a couple of days together, a week-end in New York and one in San Francisco. It wasn't enough time to develop intimacy, but it was sufficient to decide we each loved our life too much to uproot it. I think if we were truly in love, it would be different. Anyway, that's how I felt, but I wasn't sure Aaron felt the same way. Maybe he thought I'd fall in love with him and give up everything. Fat chance.

I exited the train and walked up the stairs to Canal Street and New York's Chinatown. I didn't want to venture too far from the station for fear of getting lost in the crowd. The streets were teeming with tourists and Chinese vendors hawking their wares, something that didn't happen in San Francisco. I stood and watched, absorbing the vibes.

'Hey, baby, you waiting for someone?" I turned to face a grinning Aaron, looking casual in jeans and blazer jacket.

I smiled. "What a scene. This makes my Chinatown look like amateur night."

"Yeah, it's a popular spot. Especially with women."

I couldn't accuse him of sexism, not when he was right. Women did love to shop. Particularly when they smelled a bargain.

Aaron took my arm. "How about fortifying ourselves with dim sum before we run the gauntlet?"

I agreed whole-heartedly. Dim sum was one of my favorite foods, and I hadn't had any since I'd left home.

Aaron led me to a restaurant not too far away, a small place that didn't look touristy. The customers were mostly Chinese, a sign the food was good.

We spent an hour eating delicious tidbits while we talked about our projects. I told him a little of what I'd learned from my interviews and he told me about the magazine's forthcoming issue featuring women in jazz. I was impressed and looked at Aaron in a new light. What was wrong with me? I should be crazy about this guy. He puts out an issue on women jazz players and knows how to order dim sum. And he was attractive to boot. What more could a girl want?

When we'd finished eating, we went out onto Canal Street. It was even more crowded than before. Like I said, New York was San Francisco writ large and that was certainly true of its Chinatown. The streets were lined with shops, each displaying its wares, novelties, jewelry, scarves, purses, hats and god knows what else, just like Grant Avenue at home, but more so.

As we strolled along, I gawked at the merchandise displayed in front of the shops. Every few steps, a Chinese hawker came up to me asking if I wanted a DVD, the latest movie. Or a designer handbag, LV, Coach, Prada. "What you want, I get for you."

I did want one, a Louis Vuitton, like the picture Dee had given me. I turned to Aaron. "Do you know how this works? I do want a bag and I have a picture."

"Yeah, I've been here with my mother. Show one of these guys the picture and he'll take you to a shop. To the back room. Selling this stuff is illegal, you know, so these guys take a few precautions. But not many. The cops pretty much leave them alone."

"How come?"

"'Cause every time they chase them out of here, they pop up somewhere else. Besides, people aren't that sympathetic to businesses that sell bags made for pennies in a sweat shop in China for thousands of dollars here in the States."

"Yeah, I agree with that. Otherwise, I don't think I could do it."

He smiled. "That's what my mother says."

I took the picture of the LV handbag from my purse and showed it to the next guy who accosted me. He took it and said, "You wait, I come back. Wait, okay?"

I looked at Aaron and he nodded. "We wait."

Aaron and I looked over a display of scarves, and, after a few minutes, our guy returned and said. "You follow me, walk behind, okay?"

We did what he asked. About halfway down the street, he entered a shop which displayed handbags of all styles. I didn't know much about designer bags, but these didn't look expensive to me. They looked like purses you'd see anywhere.

The guy led us to the back and opened a door you'd never know was there. It blended with the wall and had no knobs or handles. We followed him into a small space about the size of a dressing room. On the wall were handbags hanging from pegs. Designer bags, I could tell. He lifted one from a peg and showed it to me. "Your bag. The same, yes?"

I took the picture from him and compared it to the bag. I inspected the inside. The zippers worked, plus it had professional-looking stitching and a Louis Vuitton logo. It looked like the real thing to me.

"How much?"

"Fifty dollars."

I didn't know what to say. Dee had told me this bag sells for fifteen hundred dollars at Saks. But before I could answer, Aaron piped up. "Too much, let's go." He took my arm.

I was about to protest. Fifty bucks is a helluva lot cheaper than fifteen hundred. What was he doing?

"Okay, okay. Forty." The guy said.

Aaron shot back, "Make it thirty and we'll take it."

"Okay."

Aaron handed him the cash and the man put the purse into a black plastic garbage bag from a bunch stashed on the floor. And we left through the secret door into the shop and exited to the street.

I smiled at Aaron. "I can't believe it. A designer bag for thirty dollars. You were fantastic. You've done this before, haven't you." I teased.

"Yeah, I told you. My mother likes me to come along with her."

"I can understand why."

I added another skill to Aaron's list of admirable traits, bargaining.

Chapter 17

WHEN I AWOKE, my first thought was the case. I mentally went over what I'd discovered so far.

I knew that Georgia Valentine had some unscrupulous men in her life, her husband, Maurice LeBlanc, who leeched off her, and her manager, Morey Stein, who cheated her. When she was released from prison, she was clean and vowed to stay that way. Furthermore, she decided to sever her relationships with these men. She was pursued by the Federal Narcotics Agency which hoped to bust her again. As a celebrity, she was prize prey.

So I had three men with motive, Maurice, Morey and Frederic Oblenger, the head of the FNA. But what I needed now was hard evidence. I had to speak to eye witnesses, if there were any still alive. I wracked my brain wondering how I could find the names of anyone who'd been in the hospital when she died.

Who else would know but M.K., she with the prodigious memory and the humongous library? I called her and asked if I could come over. She said yes, so I got my butt in gear. I was on the subway in an hour and at Joseph Katz a half hour after that.

M.K. seemed glad to see me. We chatted a bit about some new recordings she'd acquired, then I got down to business. I told her what I'd discovered and about my need for evidence.

"Was any paperwork regarding the Feds' hospital search found in Georgia's papers? It would have been a few days before her death."

M.K. didn't hesitate. "Yes, Dan Brennan gave us all those records after he finished his book. He'd gotten them under the Public Information Act."

"Could I look at them? There's some information I need to get."

"Like what?"

"The names of the officer in charge and the nurse on duty the day of the search."

M.K. said. "It sounds like you're doing a real investigation."

I just smiled.

"I'll have to look through the papers. I don't remember those names. Can you wait here? No one is allowed in the vaults."

I sat there thinking about all I had to do. In several minutes, M.K. came back, carrying a piece of paper. She sat down and slid the paper across the table.

I couldn't believe my luck. It was a report describing the search of Georgia Valentine's hospital room on May 12, 1963.

M.K. drank her tea and watched me with a bemused look as I scanned the report.

I had to decipher the cramped handwriting, but what I made out was "FNA *claimed nurse reported drugs in room 302 of Metropolitan Hospital on May 12, 1963. Occupant, Georgia Anne Valentine. Searched room, bathroom, and patient. No drugs found. Nurse, Sheila Flanagan, age 22.*" It was signed by Jack Egan, FNA, New York.

Jesus, this was better than winning the lottery.

"This is great, M.K., I'll see if I can locate them. Hopefully, they're still around."

M.K. was silent a moment, then she said. "Have you considered the father?"

I looked up sharply. "Georgia's father? You told me about him, but I didn't think he was in the picture."

"He wasn't, not until she became famous. Then he became a nuisance."

This was the first time I'd heard this story. "Tell me about it."

"Well, he'd show up at her gigs, drunk as a skunk, and tell anyone who would listen he was Georgia Valentine's father. He was an embarrassment. Georgia was trying to be a respected artist. She didn't want some drunk raining on her parade."

This was terrific information, better than what I'd read on the Internet. "And? What happened?"

"Supposedly, Georgia told her manager, you know, Morey Stein. After that, her father stopped showing up at her gigs."

I stared at her, my imagination working overtime. "I hope you're not implying Morey had him rubbed out."

M.K. laughed. "No, nothing as dramatic as that. He probably gave him some money and told him if he wanted any more, he'd better not come around again."

I thought a moment. "But what motive would he have for killing his daughter?"

"Well, he could have thought he'd inherit some money."

"But he and her mother weren't even married. That doesn't sound very logical."

"Since when are drunks logical?"

She was right. He could have thought that. So maybe I should consider him a suspect. Christ. I was swimming with suspects, but I hadn't a single bit of evidence.

When I got back to my place, I picked up a medium tomato and cheese pizza at the place next to my apartment building. I watched a couple of crime shows and went to bed. I was almost asleep when the phone rang. It was Aaron, asking me if I wanted to come to dinner at his folks' the next night. I agreed, though I felt a little apprehensive. But I didn't know what I had to be nervous about. He wasn't asking me to marry him, for crissake.

He said. "You know about Shabbat, don't you?"

"No," I confessed.

"Well, it's a Jewish tradition to have family and friends for dinner on Friday night. Strictly orthodox Jews follow certain rituals, but my parents dropped all that and kept only the good parts, getting together and eating great food."

"Sounds good to me. Can I bring something?"

"No, no. People always ask that, it's the polite thing, but Jews don't like it. Messes up the menu."

"Okay, but how about a bottle of wine?"

"Sure, wine would be good."

"I'll bring white." I paused. "What are your folks like?"

He laughed. "Don't worry. Nothing strange about them. Dad teaches Political Science at Brooklyn University and Mom works for the Jewish Peace Alliance."

"Oh, what's that?"

"It's an organization that promotes peace between Israel and Palestine."

"Sounds important."

He laughed. "She thinks it is, but their mission is a bit quixotic, don't you think?"

"Yeah, I guess so. People have been trying to bring peace to those countries for a long time."

"The good thing about Shabbat at my parents' is the conversation never gets boring. I promise you that."

"Good, but I warn you, I'm not that up on foreign affairs."

"Don't worry. They'll do all the talking."

I laughed and also felt relieved. I don't like being put on the spot when I wasn't sure what people were talking about. And I didn't want to be vetted by a boyfriend's parents. Especially when I didn't intend to marry the guy.

We arranged to meet tomorrow at Penn Station at five. He'd call me from there.

Chapter 18

I woke up anxious. I had to get to work. My time here in New York was limited. I wanted to wrap up the case before the apartment owner came back. I couldn't afford a hotel, and I doubted the Jazz Society could either.

I went over what I had to do. I had to talk to the people at Stein and Associates about Georgia's claim Morey cheated her. And I wanted to talk to Jack Egan if he's still around, and I wanted to find the nurse who was on duty that night. And then there was Maurice Le Blanc.

I'd do an Internet search for each of them and see who I could find first.

I got up, showered and dressed, grabbed my shoulder bag with my laptop and went to my "office" down the street.

Good thing I knew how to do a people search, because finding people from fifty years ago was not easy. They change their names, their residences, their jobs, and sometimes they die. But I can go farther and deeper into the recesses of cyber space than most people can, and, after spending the entire day, found them.

Maurice was the easiest. M.K. thought he was at the Harlem Assisted Living Center and she was right. But I'd discovered that since Georgia died, he'd been married twice and arrested once for passing bad checks. He was now eighty-three and, after such a dissolute life, was probably not in very good shape.

Stein and Associates was still in business at the same address. They represented a vocalist and a quartet, neither of whom were what you'd call big. They probably worked enough in smaller venues to keep the company going.

After Morey died, his assistant Al Rosen took over the business and upon *his* death, the reins were taken up by his son, whom everyone called Rosie. The hardest to find were Sheila Flanagan and Jack Egan. Both were still alive. Jack had worked for the government in various positions until his retirement at age sixty-five. He was now seventy-five and living with his wife in a retirement community called Avalon Gardens on Long Island.

As for Sheila Flanagan, finding her was a bitch. In addition to using all my Internet search skills, I had to make several phone calls, but I finally got her. She'd married a doctor, Alexander North, an oncologist, in 1963, and retired from nursing. They had three children, had lived most of their lives in Connecticut, and now had a New York City address. Funny, most people move away from the city when they retire.

It was early evening, and the Norths were probably getting ready to go out. But I called anyway and got a recorded message. I left comments I hoped would pique Sheila's interest, saying I was a private investigator from San Francisco, looking into the death of Georgia Valentine. I put a tone of urgency into my voice, but I had no idea whether she'd reply or not. I'd give her a day and if I got no response, I'd try again.

Then I tried Jack Egan. When a woman answered, I explained I was a private investigator and wanted to speak with Mr. Jack Egan about a former case. I figured I had a good chance with him. Cops love to talk about their cases, especially the old ones. The woman told me he was out practicing his golf game, and she'd give him the message when he got home.

There was no point calling Stein and Associates this late. I'd have to wait till Monday. That left Maurice. The poor bastard was sort of a sitting duck. Living where he did, he wouldn't have much of a social life. Maybe he'd welcome a visitor. I called the Harlem Assisted Living Center and asked for him. I was told he couldn't come to the phone. I asked if I could come visit him. They asked if I were a relative, and I answered of course I was. Visiting hours were on Sunday from ten to three, so I decided to go see him then. My work done for the day, it was time to get ready for dinner with Aaron's folks.

I got to Penn Station a little before five. It wasn't anything like I expected. I was surprised by its size. It was huge, with low ceilings and a gigantic schedule board dominating the area. Lights flashed off and on as the times and platforms were updated. It was a large, boring terminal with people scurrying about like industrious ants.

Aaron called me precisely at five to tell me to meet him at Track 4. He had our tickets already. I like a man who takes control. Especially on boring stuff like getting tickets.

It took us about an hour and one transfer to get to Woodmere. We talked about the kind of jazz we liked and our favorite artists, he mentioning pianists like Bill Evans, Brad Meldaur, McCoy Tyner and Herbie Hancock, and I vocalists like Carmen McRae, Shirley Horne and Sarah Vaughn. Though our tastes were different, we did like the same kind of music, jazz.

I don't think I could fall in love with anyone who admitted to liking rap, which to me didn't even qualify as music. No melody or harmony, just a repetitive rhythm accompanying spoken, and often obnoxious, words.

Chapter 19

WE WALKED FROM the station to his parents' home along quiet tree-lined streets. This was suburbia, all right, with its sizable homes and manicured lawns, a respite for people working in the city.

The Kleins lived on a cul de sac, with a small space in front for a lawn. It looked average, not elegant or pricey.

But the exterior was deceptive. I realized the house was much larger than it looked on the outside. The foyer had a staircase leading up and one down, so the house had at least three levels.

Aaron led me straight ahead into a spacious living room where four people were standing holding glasses of wine. He introduced me to his parents, David and Sharon and their friends, Rolf and Diana Meyerson. The men kind of looked alike, with short, partly grey beards, slender builds and informal attire. The women had good haircuts and were dressed in what's called casual chic. They all looked intelligent, their faces alert and animated.

David handed me a glass of wine. Aaron and I made small talk with the group until Sharon announced it was time for dinner. We went into the dining room where we took our places at a large table elegantly set with flowers, candles and what appeared to be the good china, silver, and glassware. I was glad to see they weren't wearing formal attire like they do in British costume dramas or Aaron and I would have been relegated to the servants' hall.

Sitting between Aaron and Rolf Meyerson, I answered a couple of questions about my job, and then the talk thankfully turned to more general topics, like politics. After a short discussion confirming their liberal leanings, they started a discussion over which was the best country to live in.

Diana chose France because of its cuisine and liberal views, whereas Rolf, her husband claimed Sweden because of its social system. I wondered if this was indicative of the state of their marriage. The rest of us voted for America, whereupon someone suggested we each describe what we liked best about it.

The group responded with moans but soon was chattering in excited tones. Aaron's father, David, tapped his glass and said we should each give our answers out loud. Sharon pleaded for a few minutes to think over what she would say, which he granted.

When time was up, David called for someone to start. Aaron raised his hand, "I'm ready." Everyone looked at him.

"Jazz," he pronounced. People laughed.

His father said. "No fair. That's your job."

"Seriously," Aaron continued. "Jazz is America's most important contribution to world culture. It began in New Orleans out of a mix of different world music systems and social conditions. It evolved and spread throughout the country and the world. It's the only art form to have been created in America. And there's no question of its world importance."

Everyone clapped and murmured their approval.

Diana spoke. "Okay, I'll go next." She took a deep breath. "I'm gonna say our geography. Or maybe the word is typography? I mean our magnificent places, like Niagara Falls, the Grand Tetons, the Sierras and the Appalachians, all the mountain ranges." She paused. "And there's the Great Plains, our two oceans, and Death Valley. And Monument Valley. And the National Parks -" She trailed off.

Aaron added. "Don't forget the Gulf and the Florida Keys."

"And the swamps with all the alligators" came from David.

Rolf commented. "Leave it to my wife to come up with something apolitical. Who's next?"

I was wracking my brain trying to come up with something interesting, but all I could think of was what was wrong with the country, too much violence, crazy ideas about guns, stupid politicians, and the inequity of our economic situations. While Diana was waxing eloquent about our natural wonders, all I could think of was how we were destroying the environment.

"I got something," Rolf said, "but it's not as fun as what you guys said. I think the best thing about America is freedom of speech. We can criticize our government without fear of reprisal. In some countries you'd land in jail or be killed."

People objected and a discussion ensued on how free speech was being eroded, with Aaron mentioning how protestors were being routinely arrested. As the comments waned, David asked for the next speaker.

Sharon raised her hand. "Well, we still have a long way to go, but I'm happy that women have made great strides towards equality. When I was starting out, not that many careers were open to women. A female lawyer or doctor was rare. And the idea of a female cop was ludicrous."

Diana said. "But women still don't make the same pay as men for the same job, and we still don't have enough representation in the government. I want to see more women in Congress, and I want to see a woman president."

Several people spoke in agreement. Someone mentioned Hillary Clinton.

Sharon continued. "We're moving in that direction. I predict that two elections from now, we'll have a woman president."

David said. "I agree with you, but we'll have real equality when we elect an atheist."

Aaron added. "How about a gay woman atheist?"

"Perfect. Three in one." This from Sharon.

"Okay, who's next?" David said.

Only David and I were left. I kept quiet. Maybe they'd forget about me.

"Okay. I'll go next." David said. "What I like best about America is its good-looking women." That brought a laugh.

"What about Italian women." Aaron said. "And Swedish."

"And Indian. You seen those Bollywood actresses?" Rolf added.

"I like them, too." David had the last word.

I was next and had yet to think of something that didn't have a negative side to it.

David said. "Casey?"

My mind spun. "Okay," I hit on something I did like, something that had no negatives. "I'll say Starbucks."

They laughed and groaned. When the ruckus died down, I explained. "But listen, think about it. No matter what city you go to or even what part of this city you're in, you'll find a Starbucks. You know when you go there, you'll find a comfortable, friendly atmosphere, and if you order your favorite coffee drink, it will be made the way you like it. And you won't be rushed. You can stay all day if you want. You can do all your business, work on your computer, make your calls, or have a meeting. And all this even if you don't order a thing."

"But they charge a bundle for those drinks," Rolf interjected.

I rebutted. "But look at it this way, where can you get office space for four bucks a day?"

Aaron stepped in. "Casey's right. And Starbucks is one of our most responsible companies. They offer decent pay, health insurance and opportunity for their workers. And they do their business ethically, making certain their suppliers are treated fairly unlike Wall Mart, for instance."

Diana said. "That's true. I heard their CEO recently on television saying they plan to make their products in this country rather than take advantage of cheap labor in China or Mexico."

I breathed a sigh of relief. I'd expected to be ridiculed for my mundane choice. I hadn't intended to give a commercial for Starbucks, but it was all I could think of. And besides, it was the truth.

"Good choice, Casey." David said, concluding our game.

On the way home, Aaron talked about his parents, how educated they were, how active, etc. I wondered if I'd embarrassed him by choosing Starbucks as my favorite American thing. Maybe he would have preferred me to talk about the free market economy, or our constitutional democracy, whatever they are.

But I'm not an intellectual, and I can't pretend to be what I'm not. Plus I'm not Jewish or even religious. It's clear that he and I aren't made for each other, even though we have a few things in common. He needs to marry a nice, smart Jewish girl. If he doesn't realize that already, he will. But, no matter what happened, I hoped we could remain friends.

Chapter 20

As SOON AS I'd had my coffee and toast, this time in the apartment, I sat down on the couch to make some calls. I took a deep breath and picked up my phone. I tried Jack Egan first.

Like last time, a woman answered. When I identified myself and asked for Mr. Egan, she said. "Didn't you call the other day? I told Jack you wanted to talk to him about an old case and he was interested. Could you give me your number again? He'll probably call you when he gets in."

I gave her my number and rang off.

Now for Sheila Flanagan, or, as she's called now, Mrs. North. I took a big swallow of coffee and punched in the number.

"North residence." A woman with an accent intoned.

"I'd like to speak with Mrs. North. My name is Casey McKie."

"May I tell her what this is about?" The woman spoke good English, but with an accent. If we were in California, I'd guess Hispanic, but in New York, it could be anything from Albanian to Sudanese.

"Yes, please tell her it's about Georgia Valentine."

"Just a moment. I'll see if she's available."

If Sheila had a guilty conscience, she'd probably not come to the phone. If she didn't, I hoped she'd be curious enough to talk to me.

"Yes, hello. This is Mrs. North. How can I help you?"

Joan Merrill

"I'm Casey McKie, a private investigator from San Francisco. I'd like to talk to you about Georgia Valentine. I understand you were on duty at the Metropolitan Hospital the night she died."

She didn't speak for a few moments. "Goodness, that's such a long time ago. Why would anyone be interested in that now?"

"Well, Mrs. North, we have some new evidence and are revisiting the cause of death."

"I remember that patient quite well. She died of a drug overdose, heroin. There's no question about that."

"Yes, I know. But what we're concerned about is who gave her the overdose."

Mrs. North was silent. Finally she said. "I knew one day I'd get a call like this."

My heart skipped a few beats. Jesus, I got something interesting. At last.

"Why do you say that?"

She lowered her voice. "I can't talk now. We should meet. Where are you?"

"I'm staying in Manhattan in a friend's apartment."

"Can you meet me at Bloomingdale's, say, on Monday? At David Burke's near the entrance. They have a nice brunch. About eleven?"

"Yes, yes, fine. Bloomingdale's, eleven. How will I know you?"

"Just look for an old broad doing her damndest to look good. Of course, that describes most of the women there." She chuckled. "I'll wear a carnation."

I laughed. I said I'd see her on Monday and hung up.

I wondered what she knew. I'd be on pins and needles until Monday. I had to do something to occupy my mind until then.

I couldn't stay in the apartment and watch movies again. This was New York, for crissakes. I had to go out.

I called Aaron and asked him what he was doing.

He hesitated just a second or two. "A friend and I are going to hear a jazz violinist at the Blue Note. Why don't you join us?"

86

"You're sure? I don't want to butt in."

"Hey, if I thought you were butting in, I wouldn't have mentioned it. Let's meet in the bar at eight."

I'd been to the Blue Note before with Calvin, but that was a few years ago. It was a cool place, the best known jazz club in New York next to the Village Vanguard. It was pricey, but, hey, how often do I get to New York?

I got there a little before eight and took a seat at the bar. I ordered a glass of white wine and waited for Aaron and his friend. I didn't have to wait long, for I heard Aaron say my name. I turned around to see Aaron and an attractive brunette. I wasn't expecting his friend to be a female.

"Casey, meet Ann Schulman. Ann, this is Casey."

We shook hands and Aaron suggested we go right in, so I paid my bill and took my glass with me. I'd forgotten how small the place was. No wonder they charged so much cover. They had to make up for their small audiences. But I needn't worry about the cover. Aaron had comps, one of the perks of being the editor of *JazzBeat*. He explained that tonight's performer, Selena Thomas, was being featured in the current issue. As was his companion, Ann Schulman, who was a jazz flutist.

While we waited for the show to begin, we talked about how long it had taken for the violin and the flute to become accepted into mainstream jazz. Ann mentioned violinist Stephane Grappelli and flutist Herbie Mann as being influential in this process. I made a note to look them up. We talked a little more about jazz artists we liked, and then the quintet took the stage. I was pleased to see the percussionist was a woman, something you didn't see often.

The music was terrific, the ballads soulful and the upbeat numbers, swinging. I'd always thought of the violin as a classical instrument, very beautiful, but serious. 'Course it's used in country music, but to see it playing jazz was something else. Selena swung her butt off.

And the percussionist was wild. She used all sorts of objects in her set up, bongos, bells, and chimes, you name it, she hit it.

It was a great evening, fantastic music and interesting conversation. I was relieved not to have to talk about the case. The only downside, although I couldn't really call it that, is it was clear that Aaron wasn't in love with me. Even though I knew we had no future together, it would have been nice for my ego if *he* thought we had. He and Ann acted like friends, not lovers, but my instincts told me that this would soon change. She was the right woman for him, I could tell.

Oh, well, it was back to the drawing board for me. But I was too involved with the case to let it bother me. For now.

Chapter 21

AFTER HAVING MY continental breakfast and checking my email, I was ready to go see Maurice LeBlanc in Harlem. The name *Harlem* conjured up so much history, the Cotton Club where Duke Ellington's orchestra played for exotic black female dancers, the Savoy Ballroom, which featured battles of the big bands, and the Apollo Theater, where jazz greats such as Ella Fitzgerald and Sarah Vaughan won the weekly talent contest.

Harlem was also associated with crime and violence, but I think that period of its history may be over. I read that when Bill Clinton established his office there, it did a lot to boost the area's reputation.

The Harlem Assisted Living Center was on Lenox Avenue, about half an hour on the subway with one transfer. It was large and sprawling for a city institution. Not a lot of warmth.

I entered a small waiting room, where two middle-aged black women were sitting together. They were wearing brightly colored dresses with matching hats and purses, which led me to believe they had come from church.

On the left hand side of the waiting room placed diagonally near the hallway was a desk on which sat a metal bell with the sign *Ring for Service.* I walked up to the desk and was about to press my hand down on the ringer, when one of the women said. "We already done that, about twenty minutes ago."

I checked the time, 12:50, ten minutes till visiting hours.

"Oh, thanks. I guess they're busy." I sat in one of the chairs.

"I don't know why. Their patients ain't goin' nowhere." One of the women said. She and her companion laughed. She eyed me quizzically. "You visiting someone?"

"Yes. Are you ladies?"

The one who stared at me answered. "Hmm, mm, our auntie. I don't think we've seen you here before."

"This is the first time I've seen my friend in years."

"Listen, honey, don't be surprised if he don't know you. That happened with our auntie. She didn't know who we were when we first came."

I answered to be polite. "I hope she knows you by now."

"No, she still don't, but we come anyway, once a week, every Sunday. She seems to like it."

"That's very nice of you." I meant that.

The other woman spoke. "It's part of our good works."

"I see." I said, even though I didn't understand exactly what they meant. I supposed it was a church program.

Just then an attendant in a white uniform came up to the desk and greeted the two women. "Hello, ladies. Your auntie is all ready for you. She's in the day room."

They rose, smiled at me, and left the room. They'd raised my spirits. Unfortunately, kindness was a rare commodity nowadays.

I stood and went up to the nurse. "Hi, I'm here to see Maurice LeBlanc." She gave me an intense look, but said. "All right, Mr. LeBlanc is ready to receive visitors. He's in the day room also."

I followed the two colorfully-dressed women down the hall to a large room where about twenty residents were gathered. Ten or so men and women of advanced age sat in wheelchairs facing a large television screen. Other folks were sitting in chairs, some in groups and some alone. Three women in white dresses sort of hovered over them. The women with the colorful hats were sitting with a wizened white-haired woman near a window. The old woman was smiling and holding hands with her visitors. Maybe she knew who they were now.

I looked over the men, who were in the minority. Two men were part of the wheel chair brigade, another was sitting chatting with two women, and one was sitting alone, his head hanging down on his chest. I must be crazy, thinking I could question an eighty-three-year-old man about something that happened fifty years ago. I felt like turning around to leave, when one of the attendants spoke.

"Are you looking for someone?"

"Yes, Maurice LeBlanc. I haven't seen him for a long time, so I'm having a hard time recognizing him."

"Oh, Maurice." She smiled. "That's him there in the blue shirt." She indicated the man sitting with the two women.

I took a good look at him. He had white, close-cropped hair, and a face unlined by age. He looked to be on the thin side, with stooped shoulders. He was involved in an animated conversation with the women, who seemed more alert than the other patients. I could tell they liked him by how they looked at him, kind of flirty like.

I wondered if he told everyone he was once married to the famous Georgia Valentine. I sucked in my breath and walked over to the group. All eyes followed me. Understandably, since I was the only white person in the room. Maurice and his two companions looked up as I reached them.

"Hi, I'm Casey McKie," I spoke directly to Maurice. "Mr. LeBlanc, I'm wondering if I can speak with you for a few moments." He stared at me expectantly. "In private." I added.

The trio sat still without speaking.

"It's about Georgia Valentine." Maurice flinched and the two women moved away with a parting smile.

Maurice stood and held a chair out for me. "Please, sit, whatever your name is. Maurice will talk to you."

He directed a broad smile my way, revealing a space where a tooth should be. Otherwise, he was a handsome man.

He sighed, his eyes rolling upward, "Oh, my Georgia, there's not a day goes by when I don't think of her."

I gave him a quick look. Was he putting me on? I didn't think so, but it was an odd thing to say about a wife of fifty years ago. Especially since he'd had two wives since.

"Mr. LeBlanc."

"Call me Maurice."

"Okay, Maurice, I'm investigating Georgia's death."

He gave me a blank look. I think he was processing my statement.

"Yeah, not a day goes by -" He stared off into space.

"Maurice, do you remember her the day she died? Were you with her?"

"Maurice treated her good. Maurice knows how to treat his women." He gave me a look I can only describe as lascivious.

"Were you with her when she died?" I tried again.

"I think of her. Not a day goes by when I don't think of her."

"You loved Georgia then." I tried another approach.

Just then, a woman rolled by in her wheel chair mumbling to herself. "Goddamn it. What the hell am I doing here? I gotta get out of here. Goddamn it. How do I get out of here?"

One of the attendants fast-walked over and stopped her and turned her back to the line of chairs. "Now, Evangeline, you're fine. Let's go back with the others. Would you like a nice cup of chocolate pudding? You like pudding, don't you, sweetie?"

She used the same kind of soothing tone a mother uses with an unruly child. Evangeline smiled up at her. "Oh, yes, please. I want some chocolate pudding."

I turned back to Maurice. He grinned. "Maurice love all his women." His eyes met mine. "What's your name again?"

"Casey. Casey McKie."

He frowned. "What kind of name is that? Isn't that a man's name? Girl, you're not gonna get anywhere with a name like that. You need a new name." He eyed me speculatively. "Want me to give you one?"

"No thanks, Maurice. I like my name."

"Suit yourself, but you're not gonna make it with a name like that."

I suppose he thought I was a candidate for his stable of girls. I wasn't sure he remembered Georgia. He obviously had some form of dementia. And I wasn't gonna learn anything from him.

I stood and thanked him. He flashed me a smile. "What did you want from Maurice? You need a job?" He looked me up and down. "You too skinny, girl, and your clothes, they boring. You gotta dress sexy." His glance wandered over to his two women friends, spotted them and waved them over.

I spoke to the attendant, a nice-looking black woman of about forty. "Mr. Le Blanc seems to have memory issues. I couldn't get the information I needed."

She nodded. "You should talk to his son."

"Oh? I didn't know he had one."

"Yes, Jayvon. He comes to visit occasionally."

"Could I ask you a favor?" I dug around in my purse for my card, the one that says *CM Insurance*, for those people I don't want to know my real occupation. "Would you mind giving him my card the next time you see him?"

She checked the card and slid it into her pocket. "I don't know when he'll come by again."

"I know, but when he does."

I thanked her and left. The two colorfully-attired women were still chatting with their auntie, appearing to be having a good time.

Well, I'd met Georgia's ex, one of my prime suspects. It was hard to imagine him as a murderer. But, then, he wasn't the same person he was then. Maybe none of them were.

Chapter 22

BLOOMINGDALE'S WAS ON Lexington between 59th and 60th. I took the number two line, transferred to number four and got off at 59th. I was such a veteran subway rider by now, nothing fazed me, not the crowds, the rush, nor the lack of light.

I found the entrance to the store and went in. Directly on my right was the restaurant, David Burke's. The place was fairly full for this hour, but there were several empty seats. I glanced around for an older, well-put-together woman sitting alone, but I didn't see anyone fitting that description. All the women were sitting in pairs. I asked the hostess to seat me, telling her I was expecting someone.

I got the impression David Burke was a big deal. Apparently he had more than one restaurant in the city, but how one chef can manage more than one place was beyond me. I imagined he trained people to cook like he did. But what about the personal touch? I didn't get it.

I glanced over the other customers. I remembered a line from a book we read in high school, something about how the rich look different from other people. That's true. The women in the restaurant looked rich. I tried to figure out what made them look that way. For one thing, their hair was perfectly cut and coiffed, nothing out of place. They could probably afford to have their hair done once a week. And then there were the clothes. They were flattering and fit well. Shoes and purses matched without a tatter or scuff mark. When I considered how far I was from looking like these women, I was surprised they'd let me in.

I noticed a woman come in by herself carrying a Bloomingdale shopping bag. I didn't need to see a carnation. I knew it was Sheila North. She looked Irish with her reddish hair, fair skin and blue eyes. And she didn't look like the other women, although she was just as elegant. She exuded a sort of energy, which made her more attractive than her features would dictate. She halted and surveyed the room, her gaze eventually resting on me. She reached into her purse and pulled out a red carnation, making me smile. When she arrived at my table, I rose and introduced myself, shaking her gloved hand.

She hung her purse and the plastic bag on the back of the chair and sat, giving me her full attention.

"I hope I haven't kept you waiting. It's ridiculous how long it took me to pick out this silly scarf." She pulled a pretty blue and yellow printed silk scarf from the bag and held it up. "What do you think? Do you think it goes with my coloring?"

"I think it's very pretty and definitely goes with your coloring." I said.

She stuffed the scarf back in the bag and picked up a menu. "Have you ordered yet? I guess not. You're much too polite. My husband would have ordered already. If I'm late, he just carries on as though I weren't coming. Such a bastard." She smiled. "I'm kidding. He's really a darling, but he doesn't like it when I'm late. And I'm always late. Awful, huh?"

"Well, at least you show up."

She laughed. "That's true. Let me recommend one of their sandwich wraps if you want something light, or the large Caesar salad if you're really hungry. They'll bring us popovers, their specialty. They're delicious. And, by the way, this is on me. My husband gives me a ridiculously large allowance."

I felt like I'd been transported back to the Fifties before women's liberation, when women were subject to their husband's approval and dependent on an allowance. But she seemed to accept her lot cheerfully.

We ordered, my taking her up on her suggestion and ordering a grilled vegetable wrap, while she ordered the soup du jour. I asked for coffee to be brought right away, whereas she asked for a pot of tea.

The waitress gone, she looked at me, her expression turning grave. "So what's all this about Georgia Valentine? I remember her very well. That was before I got married, when I was a nurse. Such a long time ago."

My coffee arrived and I took a quick sip.

"I'm investigating her death. My clients don't believe she overdosed of her own free will."

Sheila trained her blue eyes on me while she thought this over. "You mean you think someone gave her the drugs?"

"Yes, that's what my clients suspect. And if it's true, I want to prove it."

"I can't imagine how you can do that. How could you prove something that happened, let's see, over fifty years ago. God, fifty years, that's so hard to believe, so much time has passed."

"The only way to prove a crime is with evidence. I have to collect it. That's why I'm asking for your help."

"I don't know how I can help. I really don't."

"You can help by answering my questions."

"Okay, I'll do as best as I can. Fifty years, oh, my god, I can't believe it."

The waitress brought our food. I hoped it tasted as good as it looked.

I can talk and I can eat, but not at the same time. So we didn't converse until we'd finished.

I began. "Sheila, why did you say you had been expecting a call about this?"

She took a sip of her tea and made a face. "This isn't hot any more. You'd think the pot would have kept it warm."

She waved the waitress over and asked for another pot of hot tea, emphasizing the word, *hot*. Another thing about the rich, they know what they like and how to get it. But she was very polite about it, calling the waitress *honey*.

"She took a deep breath." Well, I thought it was very strange she would take drugs after talking about how happy she was without them. She talked about it all the time."

"You mean to her visitors?"

"Yes, and to us on the staff. A lot of people came to see her, more than for most patients. Her husband was there often, and other people came and went."

"What about at night?"

"No, no. no one was allowed after five. Visiting hours were ten to five. They were strict about that."

"What hours were your shift?"

"Three to eleven. Oh, that was so long ago. I was so young, only twenty-two. It was my first job, actually my only job."

"You married a doctor, I understand. Did he work at the same hospital?"

"Yes, he was a resident then. After he finished his residency, we got married. A few months after Georgia Valentine's death."

"Was he in the same area of the hospital as you?"

"No, he was in Oncology."

"Was it you who found her?"

"No, she was found early in the morning. She must have had the drugs after my shift."

"So that means someone sneaked into her room sometime after your shift. Is that possible?"

She thought a moment. "Well, he'd have had to pick the right time."

I repeated. "So you think it could have happened?"

"Yes, it would be pretty easy when you think about it." She drank some tea. "All's you need to do is put on a white jacket and look like you knew what you were doing. Just like real doctors do." She laughed.

"But would a real doctor give an injection at that time of the morning? Wouldn't it arouse suspicion? You see that in the movies, but could it really happen?"

"It depends. If it was timed just right, when no one was around. Not many doctors are around at that time of night, only the residents. But the thing is, I gave her a sedative and I don't see that she would have been alert enough to have managed an injection."

Jesus.

Chapter 23

SHEILA ASKED FOR the check and said. "Shall we walk around while we talk? I always love to look around the store. Do you mind?"

Although window shopping was not my thing, I agreed. If I could keep her talking, I'd do most anything.

Just outside the restaurant was the handbag department. I remembered my purchase at Canal Street. Here was my chance to check out some real designer bags. I saw some pretty ones, green and pink and even purple. Personally, I didn't see the point of having a lot of handbags. All you really needed is one for the daytime and one for evening. And even the evening bag was superfluous. Besides, it was a hassle switching all your stuff from one bag to another. I checked the prices, and almost fell over. Some of them were over a thousand bucks. Jesus. I could understand why Dee wanted a knock-off.

Sheila was strolling and looking, thank god. If there's one thing that bugs me, it's shopping with someone who makes you wait while they linger at everything that catches their eye. We strolled through the shoe section and I marveled at the really high heels that were all the fashion. I didn't know how women could walk in those things. They were like stilts.

"So, Sheila, another nurse was on duty when Georgia died?"

Her expression turned grave. "Yes, I was there until eleven. Georgia was asleep when I left 'cause of the sedative." We'd reached an escalator. "Let's go up to the second floor. The women's section is up there."

We'd stepped on the moving stairs. "Do you remember who visited her that day?"

"Well, let me think. Her husband. He was there often. But I don't remember who else. You know, I did what I had to do. I didn't pay that much attention who was in the room. But she had a constant stream of visitors."

"Do you remember the time the police searched her room?"

"Oh, Jesus, Mary and Joseph, I sure do." We'd reached the top and stepped off. "It was about a week before she died. It happened before my shift. I heard all about it. Everybody did."

We were in the women's clothing section and I had to admit I saw some things I'd love to have. If only I could have afforded them. "What was the reaction?"

Sheila felt the material of a dress, then moved on. "Oh, my god, the reaction. It was huge. You would have thought she'd been kidnapped. There was such a furor."

"How come?"

"People thought it was horrible the police would search a sick person's hospital room. Especially when they didn't find anything. A bunch of her fans protested outside the hospital for a couple of days. The hospital directors were furious. 'Course when she died, it blew over."

"Do you know what made the cops search the room?"

"Yes, I do." She frowned. "They said I'd called them. Imagine? I was so upset, being accused like that." She halted and looked at me, her expression displaying a hint of anger. "I really liked Georgia. She was very down to earth, very honest. And she made me laugh."

"Who do you think phoned in the tip?"

She shrugged. "I don't know if there even was a phone call. That may just have been an excuse, but if there was a call, it didn't come from the hospital. It had to be from outside."

"Why do you say that?"

"Because we thought the way addicts were dealt with was all wrong. They should have been treated, not punished. They were sick, not criminals."

We were in Outerwear. I liked coats and saw a couple I'd love to have, a full-length black cashmere, and a leather jacket with fur trim, for example. I looked at the prices. Jesus, I could buy a car with that amount.

"Wasn't Georgia hooked up to an IV?"

She looked at me. "Yes, and she'd been sedated. I tried to explain that she would have been too groggy to manage giving herself a shot of heroin. But they didn't listen to me. It was as though I wasn't even talking."

"Did you try to take it to the higher authorities?"

She gave a short laugh. "I tried, but you have to realize I was a young nurse going up against all those men, doctors, hospital directors, and police. I didn't have a snowball's chance in hell of making my point."

I could understand her problem. If there are two types of males who think they're hot shit, it's doctors and cops.

My phone rang, or should I say, rumbled. I had it on vibrate. I fished it out of my bag and stepped away from the counter. Speak of the devil, it was Jack Egan returning my call. He asked what case I wanted to talk to him about and when I told him Georgia Valentine, he said. "Oh, shit, not that one."

"What do you mean?"

"It was a mess. It caused a shitload of trouble."

"Oh, yeah? Can I talk to you about it? Can we meet?"

He hesitated a moment or two. "Yeah, sure, what the hell? I get tired of playing golf every day. Where's your office?"

I explained I was based in San Francisco and had come to New York for this case, which I think impressed him. I said I was staying in someone's apartment, and it wasn't a good place to meet. I said I'd be happy to meet him anywhere in the city.

"Tell you what. I'm at the Pier 59 golf range now. If you can get yourself out here by three-thirty, we can meet at the Chelsea Brewing Company right next door."

When I hesitated, he said. "Don't worry. It's not a dump. I take my wife there and she doesn't go to joints."

I agreed to meet him there. It was one-thirty now. I had plenty of time.

I caught up with Sheila, who was checking out a gold lamé jacket.

She said in a dreamy tone. "Wouldn't this look great with black silk pants?"

"Yes, it's beautiful."

"It ought to be. It's an Eileen Fisher."

I guess that was supposed to mean something, but I didn't know Eileen Fisher from L.L.Bean.

"Guess what? That was the man who directed the Georgia Valentine hospital search. I'm meeting him in an hour."

"For heaven's sake. He's still around, eh?"

"Yeah, and he sounds hale and hearty. He plays golf."

"Well, good for him. You can tell him for me that it wasn't me who called about Georgia having drugs in her room. That was a lie." She gave a short laugh. "And I'm still upset about it."

"Okay, I will. But why would they lie and say you did it?"

"They were covering their ass, that's why. They wanted to blame somebody for their fiasco."

We walked a bit more, then I said it was time for me to go.

She said she would stay a little longer.

"If I don't bring home something more than this scarf, my husband will wonder what I've been doing all day."

I thanked her profusely and we parted with a plan to meet again. As I left Bloomies and headed for the subway station, I thought of what a valuable witness Sheila would make when and if a murder trial ever came to pass. I smiled to myself. This was the first time I'd entertained this thought.

Chapter 24

I HAD TO transfer three times to get to the subway stop closest to the Chelsea Brewery. As I walked from the subway station, I caught a glimpse of the Hudson River. This was the first time I'd seen water since I'd been in Manhattan, which was weird since it was a bona fide island, land surrounded by water.

The Brewery was part of a huge structure, just across from a boat slip. Egan said he'd gone there to practice his golf game, but I didn't see a green. Come to think of it, New York City would be the last place to have a golf course. I wondered what he meant.

Going inside, I saw why Egan's wife liked this place. It was actually quite elegant, a word one wouldn't normally apply to a brewery. It had a very high ceiling, lots of wood, and a glass wall looking out at the Hudson.

Looking around, I spotted a man at the bar who looked like he might be Egan. He was about the right age and was wearing a golf cap. He had a Clint Eastwood look, an older man who had once been good-looking. As I got closer to him, he looked up from his beer, "Casey?"

I smiled and sat next to him. "I have a message for you. From Sheila Flanagan, remember her?"

I waited to see if he recognized the name. His blank look told me he hadn't.

"She was the nurse who was taking care of Georgia Valentine when she died."

"Oh, shit. You are really opening this can of worms, aren't you?" He smiled as he said it.

"Yep. That's what I've been hired to do."

"So what did she want to tell me?"

"She said to tell you that she didn't call to report drugs in Georgia's room. It was a lie and she's still mad about it."

He held up his hands in mock defense. "Hey, I didn't have nothing to do with that. I was told to go search her room and I obeyed orders. Jesus, it's crazy to be talking about this after fifty freaking years. I was just a kid, new on the job." He shook his head. "'Scuse my manners. Wanna beer or something?"

"Beer's fine. Whatever you're drinking."

He raised his hand, and when the bartender looked our way, Egan made a hand sign indicating a beer for me.

We waited until my beer arrived before resuming our conversation. Meanwhile, I took a good look at him. He looked to be in good shape, which, to me, means he had a flat stomach. His face was tanned and sort of craggy, which, in a man, can be appealing. He looked like the kind of guy who takes charge of a situation.

Egan said. "What's the deal? Why is somebody looking into this case now? Something happen?"

I took a sip of beer. It was delicious. "Well, evidence turned up that points to Georgia being off drugs before she supposedly took an overdose. And also that she feared for her life." That was a bit of a stretch. She'd said "someone is out to get me" in her letter, which doesn't necessarily mean murder. But I wanted him to know this was a serious investigation.

"Feared for her life? What the hell does that mean?"

"That's what I'm investigating. I understand you didn't find any drugs when you searched her room."

He sighed. "That's right. That's when the shit hit the fan. The whole goddamned city got upset. *Cops raid sick singer's hospital room* and all that crap. Christ, people were even picketing the hospital."

"Well, do you blame them? It was a pretty rotten thing to do."

He looked down at his glass. "Yeah, we did a lot of rotten stuff in those days."

"What do you mean?"

"Targeting jazz players. We hounded those people."

"Yeah, you did. Why?"

He met my gaze. "For one thing, we honestly believed dope destroyed people. We thought we were doing good. We wanted to rid the world of that shit. Now, look at the country, fifty years later, we're nowhere. Worse than nowhere."

"It does seem strange, locking people up for having a joint."

"Sure as hell does. The prisons are overcrowded and for what? Pot's not as bad as booze. It's crazy."

"But, anyway, I still wonder why you picked on jazz people."

He gazed in the distance for a moment or two. "Well, jazz wasn't high class like it is now. People thought jazz was for hopheads and criminals. Especially the boss."

"You mean Frederick Oblenger?"

Egan's eyes opened wide in surprise. "You know about him?"

"Yep. He was the Edgar J. Hoover of the FNA."

"You got that right. He was a real prick."

"Was he the one who ordered the search of Georgia's room?"

"Yeah. He hated anyone who took drugs. He actually rewarded agents who busted jazz musicians and movie stars. The better known they were, the more points you got. He ran that agency like it was his little empire. And it was. The son of a bitch."

"And he had that empire a long time, didn't he?"

"Yeah, since the thirties, thirty freakin' years. And he ran roughshod over any one who opposed him. Doctors and experts told him drug addiction was an illness and shouldn't be treated like a goddamned crime, but the bastard either ignored or discredited them." He took a big swallow of beer. "Kennedy wanted to get rid of him, you know."

"Yeah, I heard that."

"Yeah, but Oblenger got his political friends to go to bat for him. But when the shit hit the fan over the Valentine thing, Kennedy was set to give him the heave-ho."

"Oblenger told you that?"

"Oh, yeah, he knew he was skating on thin ice."

"So what happened?" I wanted to see if he would tell me the same story as Dan Brennan.

"Valentine overdosed. That's what happened. That sort of vindicated his actions."

I gazed at him a moment. "So her death was good for Oblenger."

He just stared at me and drank his beer.

I said. "The nurse said Georgia had been sedated and it would have been hard for her to inject herself."

Our eyes met and held.

He replied. "Yeah, I remember hearing something about that."

"Was Oblenger capable of murder? Could he have instigated the overdose to avoid being dumped by Kennedy?"

Egan keep his eyes on his beer glass as I stared at him.

Finally, he looked at me. "I've wondered that myself. There were guys who would have done whatever Oblenger asked. But I wasn't one of them. I hated the guy. He did everything he could to hold on to that job, but murder? I dunno."

We'd come to an impasse. I didn't know what else to ask. So I asked him what he meant by practicing his golf game here. He laughed and explained it had a virtual hitting range. You stood in a stall facing a screen, selected the golf course of your choice to be displayed, then hit the balls automatically placed on the tee.

"Jesus, what will they think of next? I heard that there's even virtual hunting. You can shoot deer from home."

His eyes widened in surprise. "You mean live animals?"

"Yeah. You wait for them to pass in front of the camera, then click. Real dead."

"No shit? That's crazy. Loses the whole point of hunting, being out in nature, hunting for prey, like a mountain man."

I sighed. "Yeah, unless you just want to kill something."

When we parted, Egan asked me to keep him posted on my progress and call him if I had any more questions.

"If that asshole Oblenger really had something to do with her death, I want to know."

He was a pretty neat guy for a narc.

After almost an hour of subway travel, I got back to the apartment. Thinking of another evening alone made me homesick. At home, I always had Dee's club to go to. On impulse, I gave Dee a call. It was late afternoon in San Francisco. She might be home.

"Hello?" Her deep voice was a welcome sound.

"Hey, Dee, it's Casey."

"'Bout time you called, girl. We been wondering about you. How's New York?"

"Big." Her laugh rang in my ears. "I bought your knock-off."

"You did? Is it like the picture I gave you."

"Exactly the same. And it cost thirty bucks."

"Hot damn. I can hardly wait to see it. When you comin' back?"

"I don't know. I have this cold case to solve, remember?"

"Yeah, how's it comin'?"

"Slowly. I have lotsa people to talk to. It'll take time."

"How's Freddy?"

"He's good. Haven't seen him for a few days. I met John Beasley and his wife, Bernice. We went to the Vanguard to see the Moore Brothers."

"Oh, stop, you're making me jealous. Wish I could be there. Tell them hello."

"How's the remodel coming along? Are you ready to re-open yet?"

"Oh, shit, you know those construction workers. It always takes longer than they say. Maybe another week."

"What are you doing to entertain yourself?"

"Entertain myself, hell. I'm down there watching those mother-fuckers. Think I'm gonna leave them on their own?"

I had to laugh. I could just see her giving those guys hell.

"How's Harry?"

"Don't know, haven't seen him." She paused. "What about your boyfriend?"

I told her about going to his parents' house for Shabbat dinner.

"Meeting your future in-laws, eh?"

"Hell, no. If anything, it made me realize that we're not for each other."

"What? I thought you liked him."

"I do like him, but not enough. He needs a nice Jewish girl."

"Maybe so. Jews do stick together. You find Georgia's murderer yet?"

I laughed. "No, but I am finding out some interesting stuff."

"Such as?"

I summarized what I'd learned from Sheila North and Jack Egan.

"Girl, I'm impressed. It sounds like you're getting somewhere."

"I guess. Tomorrow I'm going to Georgia's booking agency."

"They still around?"

"Yeah, I'll let you know what I find out."

We chatted a bit more and hung up. As soon as I did, I felt lonely again.

I found an old comedy on television and watched it until I fell asleep.

Chapter 25

STEIN AND ASSOCIATES had the same office they had when Morey had the business back in the Forties. It was now run by a man known as Rosie. They seemed to have a low-key operation. I didn't find many references to them on the Internet and the artists they handled were not well-known. In fact, they were hardly known at all.

The office was in an old, small building that looked like it hadn't been touched in fifty years. I entered the small lobby and checked the company directory. *Stein and Associates* was on the second floor, along with *Triple C Bail Bond* and *Pavel Lukovic, Attorney-at-law.*

Stepping out into the dimly-lit hallway, I turned right and passed several dark-paneled doors. Neither the doors nor the walls had windows. I felt like I was in a film noir movie, about to confront an ominous killer crouching in the dark, his gun aimed at my heart.

I came to a door bearing a brass plate with *Stein and Associates* engraved in small letters. The door was unlocked and I went in, not knowing what I'd find. A heavily made-up, brown-haired woman of about forty-five was sitting at a desk filing her nails. She put down her nail file and looked up at me, as if to say "What the hell are you doing here?"

"Hello, I'm Casey McKie, and I'd like to speak to Mr. Rosen."

The office was deadly quiet. I had the feeling you get when you're in an uninhabited place. You knew no one was there. It wasn't only deadly quiet, it had no vibes.

The woman said to me in a sullen voice. "Mr. Rosen is not here. You can leave your name and number, if you want, and I'll pass them on."

"Perhaps I can wait. When will he return?"

She replied without the phony politeness one usually gets from receptionists. "I can't really say. You can't wait for him here. You'd just be wasting your time."

"So are you saying he doesn't come in? Does he have another office, somewhere I can see him?"

She sighed. "No, this is his only office."

"Okay, so what do people do when they want to see him?"

She smirked. "They call and make an appointment."

"I did call and was told, I guess by you, he was busy. So what should I do?"

"Why don't you tell me what this is about, and I'll pass the information on. If he wants to see you, he'll call you."

It was a helluva way to run a business, but I guess he had the right to screen visitors. He didn't act like he wanted clients. He was acting more like, an image came to me of Al Pacino sitting at his desk with his minions around him, the Godfather, and I don't mean some nice man acting as a surrogate daddy.

"Okay, please write this down." I gave her my card, a real one telling him I was a licensed private investigator. "Please write *Georgia Valentine* on the card. I want to talk to him about her."

The woman, her tongue slightly protruding her lips, wrote on the back of the card and placed it firmly on the side of her desk. "I'll make sure he gets it."

I bet she will. I thanked her and split.

Oh, well. Nothing ventured.

What now? I spotted a coffee shop a few doors down and hightailed it over there. I ordered a cappuccino and took it to a comfy-looking armchair. I plunked down and heaved a sigh. I felt let down. Where was I on this case? I had a list of possible suspects, each with a motive.

I had a working theory about how the murder was accomplished, but no evidence. *Zero. Rien. Nada. Zilch.*

The problem was relying on people associated with the victim. Since the crime occurred fifty-odd years ago, those people were gonna be in their seventies or eighties or dead. I need to talk to a younger generation.

Something was fishy about Stein and Associates. It looked to me like a shell office, an office in name only. It had a desk, a phone and a receptionist with nothing to do but file her nails. I needed the skinny on this operation. Where could I get it? Would M.K. know? Freddy? Dan Brennan?

Then it came to me, Ernie Garbarino, a New York cop who'd come through for me before, paying me back for a credit card fraud case I'd helped him crack a few years ago. A phony booking company seemed to be in the same category as credit card fraud, so this might be right up his alley. I still had his number logged into my phone, so I called him. It rang several times. I was about to hang up, when I heard his raspy voice. "Yeah?"

He still had a smoker's voice, only it sounded worse. "Ernie, it's Casey, Casey McKie. How ya doin'? I'm in New York working on a cold case and need some info."

"Whatcha got?" He rasped.

"Do you know anything about a booking company called Stein and Associates?"

"Booking? As in making bets?"

"No, as in hiring entertainment. I went to the office to ask some questions and it was weird. I'd swear it was a front for something."

"Whaddya know about 'em?"

"Well, it was started by a guy named Morey Stein back in the Forties. My case involves cheating his clients out of their pay, namely, Georgia Valentine."

"You mean the jazz singer? She's dead, ain't she?"

"Yeah, she died of an overdose in 1963. That's my case."

"Whaddya mean, you're looking into a fifty-year-old case of fraud?"

"No, homicide. My client wants me to find out if Georgia was murdered."

"And you think this Morey Stein had something to do with it?"

"Maybe. Just before she died, she threatened to expose him."

"The name's familiar. Was he connected to the mob?"

"That's what I heard. The mob set him up in business."

"So they may be still involved, eh? Using it as a front, is that what you figure?"

"Yeah."

He didn't speak for a few moments, while I listened to his labored breathing.

Then, he said. "You need to talk to Ryan Donovan. He's in Organized Crime. If anyone knows your guy, it's Donovan."

"Is he an okay guy? I don't want some shithead mucking up my case."

"He's okay, trust me. Let me talk to him first. He don't want to get involved with no shithead, neither. I'll give him your number."

I heard a woman's voice in the background.

"I'm coming, hold your horses." Ernie said in a loud voice.

"Thanks, Ernie, I appreciate it."

"Any time." He rang off.

Ernie was a damned good cop and he always came through for me, no questions asked. But I sure as hell wouldn't want to be married to him.

I sat there, going over what I'd learned from Sheila and Egan. Putting together what they told me, I could make a good case for Oblenger being responsible for Georgia's murder. He needed to calm the furor over his invasion of her hospital room. Her dying of an overdose proved the search was justified.

But Sheila said Georgia couldn't have injected herself, being too sedated. According to Egan, Oblenger may have ordered the search to

112

make his agency look good. But even though the guy was a fanatic, would he go as far as to kill someone to retain his fiefdom?

I hadn't learned anything from Maurice. Maybe I should talk to his son, Jayvon. Yeah, ask him if his father was a murderer. Like he'd give me an answer.

And I couldn't forget Morey Stein. He might well have wanted to get rid of someone threatening to expose his fraudulent accounting. Being connected to the mob, he easily could have had them take care of her. But did he? And how could I find out fifty years after the fact?

Chapter 26

THE BUILDING WAS as familiar as the Golden Gate Bridge, I'd seen it so often on TV, NYPD headquarters at One Police Plaza. How many actors had I seen go up and down those stairs, cross the square, eat a hot dog or drink a coffee from a local street vendor?

I had an appointment to meet Ryan Donovan there in fifteen minutes. Ernie must have given him a sales job on me, he'd called so soon after I'd talked to my cop pal. I took a good look around, my gaze lingering on the Brooklyn Bridge. I wondered if I could make time to walk across it. I'd always wanted to do that.

My turn to walk up the famous stairs. I went through the metal detector and asked for Ryan Donovan at the reception desk. The no-nonsense woman sitting there scanned her computer screen, mumbled "Room 432" and gestured toward the elevator.

Coming out onto the fourth floor, I saw a bank of windows with an entry door labeled *Organized Crime Division*. I went in to find a counter with another receptionist, although I don't know if that word is appropriate to describe the bulky bald-headed man sitting there. I gave my name, saying I had an appointment with Ryan Donovan. I don't know whether I was imagining it or not, but he seemed to give me extra eye-balling. I suppose he was trying to figure out if I were a witness, a victim, a perp, or a girl friend.

I sat in a chair and thumbed through a *People* magazine. I was in the middle of an article describing, what else? Brad and Angelina's rocky relationship, when I sensed a figure approaching. I glanced up to see not the eye-candy face of America's heartthrob, Mr. Pitt, but a clean-cut guy who looked as much like a cop as I looked like - well, Angelina Jolie. He was tall and slim, with light, longish hair, fair skin, and blue eyes. He was wearing a light blue shirt and tan slacks, a very conservative-looking dude.

"Ms. McKie?"

I rose and held out my hand. "Detective Donovan?"

"Hmm. Let's go up to my office."

We shared the elevator with several other people, a few of whom looking like they were visiting their parole officers. We didn't speak until we were sitting across from one another in a small windowless room, which I imagined was used for interrogating witnesses or suspects.

Ryan began. "Detective Garbarino tells me you came across a suspicious business."

He trained his blue eyes on me, all attention.

I told him about my visit to Stein and Associates, supposedly a booking and talent management agency, which had only one employee, a receptionist who didn't seem to have anything to do. He asked some questions and I gave him my best answers, which wasn't much. He'd probably write me off as a crazy broad.

But, to my surprise, he continued to ask questions. "And what is your connection to this company?"

I explained that I was working on a cold case, the fifty-year-old death of Georgia Valentine and investigating anyone with a motive to see her dead. I told him how she had suspected Morey Stein of cheating her, a practice corroborated by other artists on Stein's roster.

Ryan sat up a little straighter. Maybe I was imagining it, but he seemed to be intrigued by my story.

"What's the connection between this Stein and the current owners of the company?"

I explained that the current owner was the son of Morey's former associate Al Rosen, who goes by the name, Rosie.

I thought I noticed a flicker of recognition. "Have you heard of him?"

He shook his head. "I don't think so."

I had a choice, get up and leave, or press him. I think he knew more than he was letting on. "You're in Organized Crime, right?"

He gave me a sharp look. "Yes."

"Well, I heard Morey Stein was set up in business by a family." I used the jargon I'd learned from 'The Godfather' to show him I was hip.

He smiled. "What family, his?"

I smiled back. "You know what I mean, the mob, an organization of gangsters. I don't know which one, maybe the Valentes. I think they may still be controlling the business."

He displayed a slight smile. "And why would they do that?"

"As a front for their illegal activities and a place to clean their money."

He didn't answer, just kept looking at me, without expression.

"What if this were true? What would be your interest?"

My voice was firm. "If they were a shell business for a family, they sure as hell wouldn't want one of their artists blowing the whistle on them. And that was what Georgia Valentine threatened to do just before she conveniently died of a drug overdose."

"So you think she may have been murdered her to keep her from informing."

"I think it's a possibility."

"What makes you think this woman, you're talking about the jazz singer, I suppose, was murdered?"

I explained that she and everyone who visited her said she had kicked her habit. I told him about the letter she wrote expressing her fear she was being targeted.

"Hmm. If what you say is true, why did they call it a self-inflicted overdose?"

"I don't know. Maybe they were influenced by the narcs, uh, I mean the Federal Narcotic Agents. They'd searched the room a few days prior to her death. So the groundwork was laid. And she had been an addict -" I trailed off, letting him connect the dots.

"You're hinting at something, what?"

"Their search of Georgia Valentine's room caused a big stink, and the head of the agency, Frederick Oblenger, was afraid he would be dumped by President Kennedy, so when Georgia died of an overdose, Oblenger was off the hook. He stayed in the job."

Ryan gave me a long look. "So you're saying the FNA either influenced the NYPD to call it self-inflicted or gave her the overdose themselves."

He had neatly summarized my thoughts. "In a nutshell, yes."

"But you also suspect Stein's guys."

"Yes, I don't believe in putting all my eggs in one basket. You know, just in case."

He smiled. "Any more suspects?"

I blushed. He was teasing me, and I felt a little foolish.

"Yes, as a matter of fact, I do have another one, her husband."

"Yeah, well, the husband is always suspect. Which one of them do you like?"

"I'm really not sure yet. It would be easiest to suspect the family, you know, the mafia, but the other two have strong motives, and both had opportunity."

He didn't say anything, but continued to look at me.

Ryan checked his watch. "Time for lunch. I'm going to grab a bite, want to join me?"

"Sure, I could eat a horse."

'Here's the choice, the cafeteria or a hot dog stand. Sorry, no horses."

My answer was quick. "Hot dog stand."

"Glad you said that, the cafeteria has crappy food."

Chapter 27

WE EACH GOT a hot dog and a cup of coffee and carried them to a bench on the plaza. We ate fast, and, as we sipped our coffee, resumed the conversation.

"What made you go private? Were you ever a cop?" Ryan asked.

I told him how I'd gone to the Oakland Police Academy and been hired by that city's police department, but quit after a year on the job.

"Why?"

I decided not to mention my short-lived marriage to Dick Aragon, whom I had met at the Academy and who'd also gone to work for the Oakland PD.

"'Cause it was obviously an old boy's outfit and I knew I'd never get anywhere. Besides, I don't like taking orders."

He laughed. "That's a damned good reason. I don't like it either. So you started an agency?"

I explained how I'd gotten a job with Pat O'Halloran's agency and when he decided to move to Arizona, I bought the business from him.

"How long ago was that?"

"Eight years. And I'm doing all right, not getting rich, but getting by."

He smiled. "And you're your own boss."

"Yep."

He took a sip of coffee. "What's the most interesting case you've worked on?"

"Man, you ask a lot of questions." I laughed. "This come from too long on the job?"

I think he blushed. "Sorry, I guess so, but I'm really interested."

"Okay, the case I'm on now is the most interesting."

"All right. I'll shut up."

"No, I mean it. Trying to solve a death that happened over fifty years ago and which may or may not be a homicide is a real challenge."

"And you like to be challenged."

"Yes. But I also like to win."

"And you think you'll crack this case?"

"Yes, but it's gonna take some work. And maybe a little luck." I sipped some coffee. I felt a little uncomfortable. I wasn't used to talking about myself, especially with a stranger. But something about this guy encouraged me to reveal a little more than I cared to.

I said. "Now you can tell me your story. How come you became a cop? If you don't' mind my saying so, you aren't the type." A vision of my ex came to mind. "And, let me add, that's a compliment."

He smiled "So taken. Well, my father was on the force, you know. He was from a long line of Irish cops. His biggest ambition was for me to do anything but follow in his footsteps." He paused, sighed, and went on. "So I went to law school. But part way through, it hit me that lawyers were a selfish bunch, only interested in money. I thought of my dad, the pride he had in his job, and I changed to Criminal Justice."

"And how did your dad feel about that?"

"I think he was happy about it. I came to the job with a college degree, so I started from a better place than he had. That was all he really wanted."

We didn't talk for a few minutes. He and his dad seemed to be close. I felt a little sad it hadn't been that way for me and my father.

"So what's your next step?" Ryan's voice brought me out of my reverie.

"Keep digging. That's the only thing I can do."

"And what do you want of me?" I looked to see if he was being sarcastic, but he seemed sincere.

"Well, you could use your resources to see if Morey Stein did have a connection to a mob, and if so, which one? And see if they're still running Stein and Associates."

He smiled. "Is that all?"

I returned his smile.

"I'll see what I can do." He rose. "I have to get back. You walking to the subway?"

"No, I'm gonna walk across the Brooklyn Bridge."

He laughed and headed back to the NYPD headquarters.

As I walked across the bridge, I thought over our encounter. Ryan seemed very conservative, yet I was so comfortable talking to him, it surprised me. He listened and seemed interested, traits rare in a man.

Get real, girl. A guy like that is sure to be married with a couple of kids. I shook myself and concentrated on enjoying the views from the bridge, which were spectacular.

But I couldn't keep from thinking about the case. I had to find out what happened in that hospital room. If Georgia hadn't injected herself, someone else did. And there may have been a witness.

Neither Sheila North nor Jack Egan had said anything about a night nurse, the one on the graveyard shift. I assumed she hadn't played an important part in the case. Someone was so sure it was a self-inflicted overdose, they never investigated any other possibility. Why?

But maybe this nurse did see something. I had to find out for myself. The easiest way to get her name was to ask Sheila Flanagan North.

I pulled my cell phone from my bag and called her. It was about five-thirty, a good time to catch her at home. The maid, or whatever she was, answered again. When Sheila came to the phone, I explained what I wanted, information about the nurse who'd been on the late shift the night Georgia died.

She sighed. "Goodness, you're not one to give up, are you?"

"No, persistence is a big part of being a successful investigator."

"I can believe it. Well, let me think back. Her name was Donna, Donna something. An Italian name. She was young, like me. They always gave the new nurses the night shifts. As I remember, she said she didn't see anyone go into Georgia's room, and the cops accepted that. They didn't press her very much, even about the sedation. They decided Georgia injected herself or had a friend do it. But the strange thing was Donna quit the next day." She paused to take a breath. "What did she say? Let me think a minute. Oh, yeah, family emergency. That was it."

I felt a surge of adrenaline. Quitting the day after Georgia died sent up a bunch of red flags. I kept my voice calm. "Do you know where she went? Have you heard anything about her since?"

Sheila sighed. "No, I have no idea where she went or what happened to her. She and I weren't really friends. I never got to see her except the few minutes we overlapped. All I can say is she seemed a nice person."

"Do you know how I can find out where she went?"

"Maybe from the Nurses' Registry. She would have contacted them if she ever looked for another job. Pellitano. Her name was Donna Pellitano."

"Thanks, Sheila, you've been a great help."

I took one more look at the view and headed for home.

Chapter 28

IT MIGHT BE Sunday, but it was no day off for me. I had to get this case solved before I had to leave the apartment. Yesterday was not a good day in terms of moving the case forward. I'd spent the entire day trying to locate Donna Pellitano. I tried the nurses organizations in every big city in the country. It seemed this woman went underground. Who does that? People who are scared or dead. She may be one or the other, and I had to know which. I'd run out of ideas and decided to give it a rest for a day.

I was indulging myself by reading the Sunday paper. After I'd ordered my usual mocha and a chocolate croissant, I'd spotted a guy getting up from his chair and picked up his *New York Times*. So I was deep into an article about a murder in the Hamptons when my cell phone rang. I picked it up and was surprised to hear the nurse at the Harlem Assisted Living Center.

"Ms. McKie, Maurice's son Jayvon just came in. If you want to talk to him, I suggest you get over here. It's probably the only chance you'd get. He's hard to pin down." And she hung up.

That was curious. What did she mean? Why see him there? Why not see him where he lives? But she must know what she's talking about. She's probably had to get a hold of him more than once.

I grabbed my bag and got the hell out of there. I didn't have time to mess with the subway, so I hailed a cab. One thing about New York, cabs are everywhere. Within minutes, I was bouncing along in the back of a speeding taxi.

I fast-trotted into the Center and down the hall to the day room. I nodded to the nurse who'd called me and glanced around the room. It looked exactly as it had when I'd last been there, the two women with the colorful outfits sitting with their elderly auntie, only this time their hats and dresses were blue and orange instead of purple and red. The line of wheel chairs was set up facing the television set, tuned to a football game. I guessed the men dominated the remote control, even though they were in the minority. The women sat with blank faces, while the men were animated, or as animated as you can be when you're stuck in a wheelchair.

I spotted Maurice, but instead of the two women, he was sitting with a nattily-dressed man, who I assumed was Jayvon. I could tell the guy was restless, as he kept glancing around the room while his father talked. I bet he wouldn't stay long. I sat down so as not to be conspicuous. The woman I'd seen rolling around the room in her wheelchair cursing was at it again, saying the same things. "What the goddamned hell am I doing in here? Goddamn it, let me out of here. Shit." Like last time, an attendant wheeled her back to the line. Jesus, is this what Hell looks like?

When, in a few minutes, Jayvon got up and left the room, I followed. As soon as we got outside, I moved up beside him.

"Mr. LeBlanc, I'm Casey McKie, can I speak to you a moment?"

His expression was a mix of surprise, intrigue and apprehension. "Whaddya want?"

He kept walking, although he slowed a bit. "I'm a writer and I'm doing a book on Georgia Valentine. Could I ask you a few questions about her and your dad?"

"That was before my time. I don't know nothin' about no Georgia Valentine."

"You do know your dad was married to her."

He gave me a "how dumb do you think I am" look. "Yah, sure."

"Well, I'm trying to get an idea of how commercially successful she was. Did your dad receive a lot of money from royalties after she died?"

"Are you kidding me? You think I'd know shit like that?"

"Well, you know how you lived. Did you live well, or did you struggle?"

"Lissen, lady, whoever you are, I don't answer questions like that. Ain't nobody's business."

"Hey, man, I'm not asking you for figures. I'm not from the IRS. Just a one word answer."

"Okay, then will you leave me alone?"

"Yeah. One word."

"Okay, we was poor. That bum never had a fucking dime. I made my own way ever since I was a kid."

I took a good look at his clothes. They looked expensive, albeit a little flashy.

"I'd say you've done very well for yourself."

"Yeah," he grinned. "I'd say so. I got a nice little business going." He halted. "There's my car." We'd stopped next to a late model, silver Cadillac sedan. "Nice talkin' to ya."

He opened the door and got in, flashing me a big smile as he drove off. Maybe he was a lawyer or a successful businessman, but I didn't think so. I had a strong feeling he'd followed in his father's footsteps and was probably making his money off women.

If Jayvon were to be believed, his father hadn't gotten money from Georgia's estate. But if he didn't get it, who did? And does that mean Maurice was no longer a suspect?

Chapter 29

I WAS PONDERING this question as I walked to the subway station and down the stairs to the train platform. It was crowded, with a lot of people traveling on Sunday, coming and going to and from Harlem.

After waiting a few minutes, the red light flashed and we all moved toward the rail. Someone jostled me and I fell forward. I saw a flash of light and heard the rumbling of the train as I fell. *Jesus, this is it. I braced myself for the crash.*

A hand gripped my arm hard and yanked me backwards onto the platform. People crowded around, staring and saying things I couldn't understand. Then they were gone. I was alone, and I couldn't think clearly. Through the fog, I heard someone say, "Can I help you, honey? I saw what happened. Are you okay?"

I made out a black woman's face, but she seemed far away. "Let me help you. You should sit down a minute."

She took my arm, led me to a bench and sat beside me.

"Do you remember what happened? You fell toward the tracks and someone pulled you back."

"It's all a blur."

"You're in shock. Do you live far?"

"East Village. I can take the subway."

"No, I don't think you should. Is there someone I can call?"

"My bag. A card." I put my hand in my bag and my fingers found a card, Aaron's, probably. I handed it to her.

She looked at it. "Shall I call this person?"

"Please."

She pulled out her cell phone and put in the number. Her voice sounded far away. "Hello, I'm here with -" she paused and asked. "What's your name, honey?"

I told her and she continued. "Casey McKie. She's all right, but she needs someone to take her home. She had a near accident. Can you come?" She listened a moment, then handed the phone to me. I heard a male voice, but I couldn't make out who it was or what he was saying.

I handed the phone back to the woman, who said. "She's not hurt, just shook up. I'll wait with her until you come. We're at Platform Three."

We sat there without talking, the woman rubbing my arm all the while. My mind was slowly clearing. It was like being high on booze or drugs, nothing seemed real. Everything was far away.

Little by little, my mind cleared, until I could see the woman sitting by me. She was about my age and nicely dressed, like a business woman. "I must be keeping you from something. I'm so sorry."

She smiled. "Don't worry, honey. So I'm a little late getting home. It's okay." She looked at her watch. "Your friend should be here soon. How do you feel?"

"Very weird. Like coming off a high. But everything is coming into focus. What happened? Did I faint?"

"No, you fell toward the rail." She shuddered. "But a man pulled you back, thank the lord. He didn't stick around, though. He probably figured you were okay."

"I didn't hit my head or anything?"

"No, you're in shock. I've seen that reaction before. It is like being high, but it'll wear off. You'll be fine."

I remembered how crowded it had been before I - *Jesus, that was close.* "I think someone pushed me."

"Now, honey, don't think that way. It was very crowded and you prob'ly lost your footing. People don't push folks onto the subway tracks. It was an accident. Lucky you're not hurt."

I didn't answer her. But I knew better. Instead I asked her name.

"Cora, my name's Cora Williams." A man approached us. "I think your friend is here."

I looked up. It wasn't Aaron. It was Ryan Donovan. He sat beside me. "What happened?"

Cora answered. "She fell toward the tracks and someone pulled her back. She's shook up, but she seems to be getting better."

He said to me. "Fell toward the tracks? How could that happen?"

Cora said. "It was crowded."

Just then a train pulled up. "I better go. You'll see her home, won't you?"

Ryan rose. "Of course, thank you. That was very kind of you."

I understood she was leaving. I stood and gave her a hug. "Yes, Cora, thank you, thank you."

"My pleasure. You take care now." And she was gone.

Ryan sat down again and put his arm around me. "Are you okay?"

I leaned into him. "Someone pushed me. I know it."

My mind cleared, and my feelings came rushing back. I pulled away from Ryan, embarrassed. What must he think my calling him to come get me, when I barely knew him? I must have pulled his card from my bag, thinking it was Aaron's. But I was glad for my mistake. I think I would have felt more embarrassed if it were Aaron. I didn't know why.

"I don't know who pushed me, but I've been stirring the pot all over the place."

"You're sounding more like yourself. Come on, let's get out of here. You need a drink. There's a place a couple of blocks from here."

The Lenox Lounge didn't look like much from the outside, but inside, you felt the vibes of history. We walked through the bar area to the Zebra Room in the back. One look at the décor explained the name. It was like entering an entirely different place from the crowded and noisy front room. It was quiet and cozy, with a tile floor and vinyl booths. I felt like we had stepped back in time.

After a couple of swallows of brandy, I felt better. The shakes and chills were gone, and my brain was beginning to function. I told Ryan about the mix up with the cards and how embarrassed I felt.

"Hey, I'm glad it happened. This is much more exciting than the game I was watching."

"But your family must be wondering -"

He held up his hands. "Not to worry on that score. I live alone." He took a sip of his drink. "So tell me exactly what happened."

I was surprised at how happy I was to hear that he lived alone. *Stop it, Casey, you're on a case and he's a source.*

I took a deep breath. "I was waiting on the platform. It was crowded. People were bunched up waiting for the train. I felt a shove and fell forward. I remember thinking I was about to die. I felt a hand grab my arm and pull me back. That's about all I remember. I came to sitting on the bench with Cora." I looked him in the eyes. "What a nice woman, waiting with me like that. It must have been at least half an hour."

"You really think someone shoved you?"

"Yes." I was relaxed enough to look around. "Hey, this is a cool bar."

Ryan gestured toward the room. "Yeah, the Lenox Lounge has been here forever. It's a jazz joint, but lately they've been bringing in R&B and other music." He made a face. "Gotta make ends meet."

"Are you into jazz?"

"Sure, I like jazz, and blues, Latin, R&B, some rock, country. You?"

"Yeah, the same. My best friend is a jazz singer who has her own club near my apartment."

"Really? Great hang out for you, I bet. San Francisco, right?"

'Yeah, you been there?"

"Couple of times. Love it." He took a swallow of brandy. "Okay, who do you think shoved you?"

I shrugged. "I wish I knew, but I may be getting too close to the truth for some people."

"Like who?"

I told him about talking with Jack Egan, Sheila, and Maurice's son, Jayvon. "I more or less asked each of them if they had anything to do with Georgia's death."

"Not to mention the Stein Agency." He smiled. "Did you come out and accuse them of murder?"

I smiled back. "Not exactly, just asked them a few questions. But, get this, I found out the nurse who was on duty when Georgia died quit her job the next day. And she seemed to have dropped off the face of the earth." I told him about my all-day search.

"Now that IS interesting." He met my gaze.

We talked a little more, had a second drink and I started to yawn. Apparently, shock is followed by lethargy.

Ryan insisted on driving me back to the apartment. We walked a few blocks to pick up his car at a garage. We didn't talk as we drove to my apartment.

Ryan said he wouldn't try to park again, so he drove down Third to the front of my building.

I yawned, thanked him and reached for the door handle. Then I stopped short. "Jesus, look at that."

Ryan leaned toward me to look at the entry door.

Go home bitch had been spray-painted in large black letters across the blue door. Ryan sucked in his breath. "Who knows where you live?"

"I didn't think anyone did. Someone must have followed me."

Ryan's tone was wry. "Or had you followed. Christ. I'm taking you home with me. You can't go in there."

I was too shook up to argue.

Chapter 30

RYAN SHOWED THE attendant his card and we drove into the garage. He parked the car and led me to the elevator, which had a security card slot.

I was impressed. "Man, you got some security here."

Ryan smiled. "Yeah, this used to be a safe house. In fact, I think the department still uses one of the apartments for that purpose. They insist on security." He gave a short laugh. "They've invested so much time in me, they don't want some wise guy knocking me off."

"Ha. Ha. In other circumstances, that would be funny."

"Sorry. Gallows humor, I guess, comes with the territory."

We'd reached his floor. The door opened to a short hallway with only one door. He opened it with his card and we entered a spacious living room.

Ryan looked at me. "Listen, I don't want to alarm you, but if someone from a family is out to get you, you're gonna need all the protection you can get."

I sighed. "I wish I'd brought my Beretta, but I didn't want the hassle of getting it through airplane security."

"I can lend you a piece if you'd feel safer."

"Jesus, you think I'm in that much danger?"

We'd stopped in the middle of the room.

He looked at me. "I don't really know, but you have to remember, I deal with guys who don't think twice about killing people. And if you're right about what happened on the subway -" he trailed off.

"Yeah, and don't forget the nice message on my door."

"We're not sure it was meant for you, but to be safe -" His face brightened. "How about a drink?"

I yawned again. "In a minute. Right now, I just want a shower."

Ryan moved toward a hallway to the left. "Your room is down here."

His guest bedroom reminded me of a standard hotel room, double bed, dresser, table, chair, lamps, an innocuous picture above the bed. Nothing personal.

He opened a door. "Your own bathroom."

"This is great. I'll take it."

He laughed. "I'll give you half an hour and then I'll see you out here for dinner. I'm cooking, but don't expect too much." He left, closing the door behind him.

Jesus, I can't believe this is happening. I felt like I was in a movie. Everything seemed unreal, the subway, the warning on my door, ending up in this apartment with a man I'd just met. Maybe it was a set-up. Maybe Ryan was the one trying to bump me off. I had to laugh at myself. I'd seen too many crime movies.

After showering and dressing, I emerged and entered the living room. Ryan called out from the kitchen. "Help yourself to the wine."

I poured a glass of red wine from the bottle on the coffee table and took a good look around. This was no ordinary apartment. It looked expensive, spacious and well-furnished. But, like the guest bedroom, it was impersonal. No photographs, no knick-knacks of any kind.

I walked over to the window and looked out onto what I supposed was the Hudson River. To the left at some distance was a bridge, must be the Brooklyn.

"How do you like my pad?" Ryan walked out of the kitchen carrying his glass.

"How'd you rate a place like this? Are you sure you're a cop and not an investment banker?"

He laughed. "It's a perk of the job. It belongs to the department. As I said, it used to be a safe house, but they hadn't used it for a while. They may kick me out any moment."

"It's fantastic. The perfect New York apartment."

"What's your apartment like, in San Francisco, I mean?"

"Well, it's in Chinatown, which is a miniature version of yours, without all the hustlers. And right next to North Beach, which is our Little Italy. It's a cool neighborhood. I love it. I can walk everywhere."

"Sounds great. I envy you. I like that city. New York can get to be too much." He took a sip of wine. "Ready to eat?"

"Damn right. I'm starving."

He'd made a salad, steak, and mixed veggies, a respectable dinner. We talked while we ate, mainly about our jobs. I explained how my bread and butter work was with a law firm, consisting mostly of boring background checks. He told me of all the reports he had to fill out. We both avoided talking about the hairy aspects of our jobs, the parts we lived for. And neither of us said a word about previous marriages or romances.

I yawned a couple of times. Ryan said. "What are you doing tomorrow? I'll be out of here eight-thirty. You'll have the place to yourself."

"I'm gonna keep looking for the night nurse. I decided to call all the Pellitanos in New York. I have no idea how many there are, but with over eight million people in the city, I imagine it will keep me busy."

He laughed. "Have fun. Help yourself to anything in the kitchen."

"Mind if I leave the dishes until tomorrow morning?"

"Nope. Good night. Sleep well." And he walked toward the hallway on the right side of the room.

Chapter 31

WHEN I AWOKE, it was a little after nine. I'd slept through. At first, I wondered where the hell I was, but after a few seconds, my mind cleared. I remembered the events of yesterday, but it was like trying to remember a dream, at least everything after I nearly fell into the subway tracks.

I didn't want to contemplate what would have happened if that guy hadn't pulled me back. I'd been lucky, and I decided to let it go at that. The spray paint on my door didn't seem so ominous this morning. It could have been meant for someone else in the building. If it were for me, painting on the door meant the culprit didn't know which apartment was mine. The front door was fairly secure, with a key lock and an intercom system. So I was pretty safe there, so long as I didn't let anyone follow me inside. I didn't have my gun, but I had my aikido skills, which needed a tune-up. Today I'd find a studio and get a workout.

I stretched. Jesus, it's good to be alive, no matter what. I mustn't forget that. I got out of bed and headed for the bathroom. After getting dressed, wishing I had fresh clothes, I went out to the kitchen. I knew Ryan had gone because it was dead silent. I noticed he'd done the dishes. Was he being considerate or was he simply obsessive-compulsive. Did it matter?

I spotted a note on the counter.

Good morning. Help yourself to whatever. I work till 5.
See you later, R.

I opened the fridge and found a bottle of V-8 juice, not my favorite, but good for you. I poured myself a small glass and drank it down. Rummaging through the cabinets, I found a box of shredded wheat, the world's most boring cereal, poured some into a bowl and added milk.

I took the cereal over to the window and looked out. The view was fantastic, the river and the bridge. I wondered why they had such an elegant apartment as a safe house. Maybe the people they'd had to keep safe were VIPs.

As great as this place was, I had to get out. I felt trapped. What was I supposed to do, stick around here waiting for my man to come home, get all dolled up and have dinner ready? To hell with that. I had to get back on the case.

I added to Ryan's note:

Gone home. Thanks for everything.

As I left his building, I checked my map to see where the hell I was. It wasn't all that far from NYPD headquarters. I could take the subway back. I wasn't gonna let some goon intimidate me. I'd keep an eye on people around me and stay away from the tracks.

But just to be safe, I decided to get a disguise. I stopped at a street stall and bought a cap. Then I found a used clothing store and picked up a lightweight, all-purpose trench coat. That should confuse anyone looking for a reddish-blonde with short hair wearing a black leather jacket. I didn't look very fashionable, but, hey, tacky was better than dead.

I went down the stairs of the nearest subway station, doing a one-eighty all the way down and avoiding the crowds. The subway car arrived and I waited until the last moment to hop on, not getting too close to anyone. Once inside, I stood apart and watched the passengers around me.

When I arrived at my building, I noticed the spray paint had already been removed. I wondered if there were a graffiti removal service in this city. If so, they had one helluva good business.

I looked around before using my key and took the stairs instead of the elevator. I opened my apartment door very slowly, alert for a possible attack. But, all was quiet. Everything seemed to be where it was supposed to be. I breathed a sigh of relief. It was good to be home, even though it wasn't mine.

The first thing I did was take a shower and put on fresh clothes. Then I found the phone book and checked the listings for the name Pellitano. There weren't as many as I thought, eighteen. But I didn't want to do my calling in this tiny space. I'd go to my second home down the street, where I could go online.

At Starbucks I got a mocha and croissant and picked a chair in a corner where I wouldn't disturb people by talking on my cell phone. I'd be considerate even if other people weren't. I'd made a list of the Pellitanos and began at the top. Of course, most of them weren't home. I left a message saying I was from American Mutual Insurance and was looking for Donna Pellitano, who had worked as a nurse in New York in the early Sixties. I may have some money for her, I said. The mention of money always got people's attention. I reached a couple of people who said they didn't know any Donna Pellitano.

I was frustrated, feeling I was wasting my time, which I hated to do. But, logic told me I had to do this. What other way would I find her? That led me to wonder what I'd do if I did find her. I shook off my pessimism. One thing an investigator has to have is faith, or maybe it was hope, that if you looked long and hard enough, you'd find what you were looking for.

I finished the list, having reached only five of the eighteen names on the list. None of them knew Donna Pellitano, but maybe one of the others did and would call me back.

I sat there for a few minutes, wondering what my next step should be. I decided to check on Dee. I hadn't talked with her for several days. It was four here, early afternoon in San Francisco.

"Hello," she sounded grumpy.

"Hey, Dee, it's Casey. How's it going?"

"Don't ask. Those lazy motherfuckers work like snails." She heaved a sigh. "But how are you doing? How's the case coming along?"

I wouldn't tell her about my brush with death. It would only make her feel worse, so I played it upbeat. "Good. I have some very strong leads. Kind of amazing given how cold a case it is."

"Tell me. I need some cheering up."

I told her what I thought was the most interesting thing I'd learned, that the night nurse had disappeared the day after Georgia's death.

"I saw something like that on one of my TV shows. A witness was bumped off and dumped into a lake. Do you think that's what happened to her?"

"Could be. Only here it would be on a deserted roadside in Long Island." I teased.

"Shee-it. I read about all those bodies of prostitutes being found. I hope you're being careful."

"Well, so long as I don't take up work as a hooker, I should be okay."

"I see you're still a smart ass. So you think the nurse saw something?"

"It's possible. Or maybe it's just a coincidence. We'll see."

Dee changed the subject. "Have you seen Freddy?"

"No, but I should call and give him a report."

"When you coming home?"

"No idea. I have to wrap this up before I can leave."

"But what if you don't? You can't stay there forever."

"No, and I don't intend to. I'll figure it out. Don't you worry."

"I know you will, girl. I better get back and see what those lazy motherfuckers are doing."

"Okay, I'll talk to you soon."

"Take care now. New York is a dangerous place, don't forget."

If she only knew.

Chapter 32

I STOPPED AT the pizza place next to my apartment and got a medium tomato and cheese to go. Then I went to the movie rental shop a few doors down and looked for a comedy. I spotted a Robin Williams movie that made me laugh every time I saw it.

I took everything up the stairs, being careful I wasn't followed. I sighed with relief once I was inside with the door bolted. I was more tense than I would admit. Before I could dig into the pizza, my phone rang. It was Ryan.

"Hey, why did you leave? I thought you were gonna stay here for a while. To be safe."

"Your place is great, but I have to keep on the case. I couldn't work there. I needed my lap top, my clothes, you know."

"Are you okay, though?"

"Oh, sure, the spray paint is gone, so all is as it was. I'm home now ready to eat pizza and watch a movie."

"Sounds good." He hesitated. I hope he wasn't gonna ask if he could come over. He'd come to my rescue, yes, but that didn't mean we had to be attached at the hip.

He continued. "I spoke to some guys here about Stein and Associates, asked if they'd heard about any mob involvement. One guy thought the name was familiar and promised to look into it. I may have an answer in a few days."

"Fantastic, I really appreciate it. You know, Ryan, this is looking more and more like a mob hit, getting rid of a witness and all."

"Yeah, I see what you mean. Any luck locating the nurse?"

I explained I'd left lots of messages, and the few people I did speak to had nothing for me.

"Good. Okay, then. I'll call you if I hear anything. And, for crissake, watch your back."

"Will do." We hung up.

What was going on with Ryan and me? Something was brewing, I could feel it. But we were both being cautious. At least I was. Maybe he wasn't interested. But I didn't have time for romance right now, not when I was on a case.

I'd finished my dinner and was laughing at Robin Williams when my phone rang again.

"Casey McKie." I answered in my professional voice even though it was long past business hours.

"Did you call me today asking about, umm, Donna Pellitano?" The voice was a woman's. She sounded mature, but not old.

My heart skipped a few beats. "Ye-s-s-s?"

"You said she might have, umm, some money coming?"

"Yes, it's a possibility, but I need to be sure I have the right person. Do you know a Donna Pellitano who was a nurse in the Sixties?"

"Well, umm. It sounds like my aunt. She worked as a nurse then. It was before I was born."

My pulse was racing. "Did she work at the Metropolitan Hospital by any chance?" I held my breath.

"Umm, I don't know the name of the hospital, but it was in New York City."

"Did she quit abruptly, do you know?"

She paused. I began to worry. Maybe I shouldn't have asked that. Maybe I'd given too much away.

"Umm, I dunno. All's I know is she moved to Florida all of a sudden."

"Where is she now?"

I held my breath. I felt like a defendant awaiting the verdict of the jury.

"Well, she's, umm, back home. She came back a few years ago after her husband died."

"Where's home?"

The woman hesitated. "Umm, I don't think I should give out her information, but I can give her your name and number." She paused. "Why do you want to talk to her?"

Should I continue with my lie about the insurance or tell her the truth? I went for the truth. "Please tell her I'm a private investigator, please emphasize *private*, looking into the death of Georgia Valentine. And tell her she can trust me."

Her voice was subdued. "Okay, I'll tell her."

We hung up and I tried to get back into the movie, but I couldn't. My mind kept going over various scenarios. One of which was that if this woman was not legit, I had just shown my hand to the wrong person.

I was depressing myself, so I turned on the movie again and pretty soon I was laughing.

I was almost to the end when my phone rang. Jesus, this is late to be calling. I hoped no one was dead.

"Hel-lo?" The voice was female, older. And she sounded querulous.

"Yes, hello. This is Casey McKie, can I help you?"

Christ, I sounded like Customer Service.

"Are you the person looking for Donna Pellitano?"

I sat straight up, adrenaline pumping.

"Yes, ma'am. Are you she?"

She chuckled softly. "Well, my name used to be Pellitano a long time ago. Now it's Corelli, Donna Corelli. What do you want with Donna Pellitano?"

"If she worked at the Metropolitan Hospital in 1963 and was the night nurse for Georgia Valentine, I have some questions for her."

Silence. After a few seconds, she spoke again. "What kinda questions?"

"Some very important questions, on behalf of people who want to know the real circumstances of her death. These people honor Ms. Valentine as an artist and want to make sure her legacy isn't tarnished by a lie."

"And what would they do with this information, if they got it?"

"They would tell the world the truth. They're not interested in vengeance or retribution. They're not associated with the law or the media. They're artists, jazz artists. They only want to clear Georgia Valentine's name."

She was silent. I could hear her breathing. "What do you mean by 'clear her name?'"

I took a deep breath. "They don't think Georgia took an overdose of heroin. They think someone else injected her. Murder, in other words. They want her name to go down in history as a great artist, not someone who gave in to drugs."

Silence, then. "I see. I can help you, but -" She hesitated. "You have to promise me that my name will not be used. You have to promise that, or -"

To say I was elated is an understatement. "Yes, yes, you have my word. Can we meet?"

"Yes, all right."

"Any time and place you say. I'm in Manhattan. Where are you?"

Silence again. "I'll meet you at St. Patrick's at eleven tomorrow."

"Perfect. How will I know you?"

"I'll be sitting in the second row on the left side, my usual place. I'll have on a black head scarf. Sit in front of me and don't turn around. I don't want people to know I'm talking to you."

"Okay, see you then." She sounded like she was practiced at being underground.

Wow, I felt like doing a dance right there in that dinky apartment. Now I was getting somewhere. I wanted to tell someone. Ryan? No, I'd given my word to Donna and I couldn't trust him to keep quiet. This was one promise I intended to keep. I had to keep the good news to myself.

Chapter 33

I GOT UP early, with the anticipation you feel when something good is about to happen. I showered, put on a skirt and blouse, my new coat and cap. I looked like a holdover from the Sixties, but that's okay, if it kept me safe from hit men. I went down to Starbucks and had my usual breakfast. I checked my map and got the route to the Cathedral. On the way down to the subway platform, I stopped to listen to a jazz saxophonist and dropped a buck in his case. This platform wasn't as busy as the one in Harlem, but still, I stayed back from the rails and scanned the people waiting for the train.

I made it to my stop without incident and walked to the Cathedral. It looked like it had been lifted from Fifteenth Century Italy and squeezed into this spot. It was dwarfed by its neighboring skyscrapers, its spires reaching heavenwards, like shaded plants seeking the sun.

It was apparently a tourist attraction, for people were wandering around gazing at the stained glass windows and generally looking awestruck. Worshippers were scattered throughout the pews, mostly alone, their heads bowed. I spotted a woman in the second row, her head covered by a black scarf. Donna.

I walked slowly, glancing around, doing my best to act like a tourist. When I got to the front row, I took a seat a little away from her and took a good look at the church. It was beautiful, with hundred-foot ceilings, arches, pillars and stained glass windows. Statues stood in naves and votive prayer candles flickered everywhere.

I kept up my act for several minutes, until I began to wonder if I was sitting in front of a stranger instead of Donna Pellitano. Then I heard a voice whisper. "Ms. McKie? Is that you? Nod, don't turn around."

Jesus, either she was paranoid or really scared. I nodded and bowed my head as if in prayer.

She spoke softly. Anyone watching would think she was saying her novenas. "Funny, I remember it like it was yesterday. They called and told me to leave my station at midnight for twenty minutes. If I didn't, I'd be very sorry. I thought they wanted to talk to her. I didn't know that they, uh, what they would do."

I heard the emotion in her voice. "When I got back, I didn't see anyone 'cept a nurse coming down the hall. I looked in and Georgia seemed to be asleep. I wondered if they had even been there. I didn't think anymore about it." She paused. "But later, when I brought Georgia's meds, I couldn't wake her. I called security and they called the police. When they asked me if I'd seen anyone, I said no. I said I'd only left to go to the bathroom. They decided Georgia had given herself the injection."

She hesitated and didn't speak for a few moments. "But anyone could have given her drugs. She has lots of visitors. I told them she had been sedated, but the main cop didn't pay any mind." She paused. I didn't move a muscle. "The next morning I got a call. The voice was all distorted, but I understood what he said. I had a choice. I could get twenty thousand dollars if I moved away from New York. If I didn't move, they couldn't guarantee what would happen to me and my family. I believed them. I knew what the Sicilians do to people."

She sighed. "I called the hospital and said I had a family emergency and couldn't come in. Later I received a special delivery package with the money. I packed up and moved to Florida and told my parents not to tell anyone where I went. I didn't tell them why. I didn't want them to know anything."

She paused again. "I changed my name and got a job as a nurse in a retirement home. After a few years, I got married to a very nice man and had two kids." She took a deep breath. "I had a good life and almost forgot about what happened." Her voice was strained. "But I never stopped thinking I'd helped kill that woman. I've prayed for her every day of my life.

"When my husband died, I came back home. But I'm still afraid, especially now that people are looking into the case. Those Sicilians." She spit out the word. "They don't forget. And I don't want to go to prison. I'm old. I want to live a quiet life and enjoy my grandchildren. Do you understand?"

I nodded slightly. I wanted to answer her, to ask more questions, but I had to respect her caution. Remembering my "accident" at the subway and the message painted on my door, I figured maybe she wasn't being so paranoid.

"I'll call you. Please leave now."

I took one more look around the church, got up slowly and walked down the aisle, avoiding even a glance at Donna.

My mind was whirling. Jesus, what a story. This will probably be the best evidence I'll get that Georgia Valentine was murdered. And by someone from the mob. But which mob? And which hit man? And by whose orders?

That's what I had to find out. Donna couldn't help me. She didn't see the person who threatened her. But even if I did find out who it was, I couldn't make a case. Donna wouldn't testify and I had to keep her story to myself. But now I knew for sure that Georgia had been murdered. I knew how and when it was done, but I didn't know by whom. Only that it was a hit man or someone giving a good imitation of one.

My next step was to talk to the cops, if any of them were still around, and find out why they ignored the information about the sedation. And how it might have prevented her from injecting herself.

144

Why didn't they pursue that line of thinking? Did they know the night nurse had quit? Did they even care?

These thoughts spun in my brain like leaves in the wind, and I had a hard time concentrating. I'd forgotten I was on high alert and did a quick scan of my surroundings. People were coming toward the church, some worshippers and some tourists, but none of them looked like an assassin. But then what did an assassin look like?

I spotted a small café down the street about half a block.

I needed to sit down over a cup of coffee, calm down and do some serious thinking.

I got a cappuccino and sat down by the window. I wondered what Donna's life had been like. She said it had been good, but she'd never been entirely free of guilt or fear. Maybe being in Florida tempered these emotions. I tried to put myself in her shoes. Had I been given her choice, would I have done the same thing? She understood the seriousness of a threat from a Sicilian mobster.

But why did they give her money when a threat would have sufficed? Because taking money incriminated her and was added insurance she wouldn't talk. Could she be prosecuted if the case were taken to court? Probably. People have been convicted for less. I wouldn't risk it. I won't tell her story, at least not in a way that would lead anyone to her.

I wondered where I could get the name of the cop she spoke about. From the Joseph Katz Collection maybe. That would be the place to start. I wouldn't dare ask Ryan. A cop couldn't or wouldn't keep a story like that quiet.

Chapter 34

I CALLED M.K. but she was out to lunch. I decided to go over there anyway. I was hoping the hospital paperwork would be in the archives. If not, well, I'd have the pleasure of another ride on the subway and another chat with M.K.

With my sunglasses, my cap pulled over my forehead and my Monk-style trench coat, I didn't look like the same woman who was shoved into the subway tracks, but, nevertheless, I was cautious, eyeballing everyone I passed on the street and at the station. And I sure as hell kept away from those goddamned tracks.

I got to the Joseph Katz building about forty minutes later, hopefully in time to meet M.K. returning from lunch.

I went in and asked for her. In a few minutes, she came out to the lobby sporting a big smile.

"Hey, M.K., what are you looking so happy about?"

She laughed. "I know, yeah. Well, I went to a collector's swap this week-end and scored big time."

By "score," I bet she wasn't referring to drugs or sex.

She explained. "I got some vintage Art Pepper and Clifford Brown recordings I've been wanting for a long time."

"That's great. What's a collectors' swap?"

"A bunch of jazz geeks like me get together and talk about their collections. We trade rare stuff." She gestured for me to follow her to her office.

Once we were seated at her desk, I told her what I wanted. "I've been talking to people about Georgia's death, and I'm getting closer to knowing what happened."

M.K.'s eyes widened. "What?"

"Well, I want to wait until I have the complete picture, but I can tell you that what people suspected is true. She didn't kill herself, either accidentally or deliberately."

M.K.'s expression turned serious. "You mean she was murdered."

"I think so."

"By whom?"

"Well, that's the big question, isn't it? I know how and when it was done, but not by whom. More than one person had means, opportunity and motive. But which one of them did it? I don't know. Yet."

"What are you looking for in the hospital records?"

"The names of the cop who came to the hospital the night she died. Do you have that?"

Her face became animated. "We might. We got a couple of boxes from the hospital a while back. They'd transferred most of the records to an electronic file and wanted to dispose of the hard copies. They were gonna burn everything, but they knew we held Georgia's papers, so they called us. Thank god, huh?"

"No kidding. So it's all in boxes?"

"Yes, I haven't had time to go through them. But, tell you what, I'll bring the boxes down and we can go through them together. You got time?"

"Damn right I do. Can I help you carry them?"

"No, thanks, I'll get a cart. Want some coffee while you wait?"

She poured me a cup from an electric pot on a side table and left.

I sat there drinking her too strong coffee, going over again what I'd learned so far. The story had holes I needed to fill in. What it boiled down to was evidence. I needed proof, hard to come by in a fifty-year-old crime. And if I couldn't get proof, I needed the alternative, a confession.

M.K. arrived pushing a cart with two boxes of papers. We each took one and set it on the floor next to our chairs. The papers seemed to have been dumped into the boxes in no particular order. They were loose, no neat file folders. So we had to look at each sheet.

We got faster as we went along. We figured out where the date was located and checked that spot, looking for May 17, 1963. It became rote enough to allow us to talk. 'Course we talked about jazz. Who were our favorite musicians? Vocalists?

M.K., being the true aficionado, liked Miles Davis, Charlie Parker, Lester Young, Dave Brubeck, while I, a sometime fan, named Gene Harris, Les McCann, Regina Carter, Stephane Grappelli, none of whom were what you'd call hard-core jazz. When it came to vocalists, I was on more solid ground. I mentioned Carmen McRae, Sarah Vaughan, Ella, Anita O'Day, and Johnny Hartman for starters. It was fun and helped relieve the boredom of our task.

Two hours and a pot of coffee later, we found the paper we were looking for. It was a note on Georgia's chart for May 17, 1963, stating: *"Deceased. Cause of death: drug overdose. Officer in charge: Sergeant Mike Donovan, NYPD."*

It took a second for it to hit me – *Donovan*. Ryan's father was a cop, he'd said. Was Mike Donovan his father? If so, why hadn't Ryan mentioned it? What was going on?

If M.K. noticed the expression on my face, she probably chalked it up to my happiness over finding the chart. And I wasn't about to tell her about Ryan Donovan. But I could hardly wait to get out of there so I could call him.

M.K. made a copy and gave it to me. We put the papers back in the boxes and placed them on the cart. We said good-bye and M.K. pushed the cart towards the elevator.

As soon as I was outside, I called Ryan. I got a recording and left a message for him to call me as soon as possible. Then my imagination took off. Did Ryan have a vested interest in the investigation? Would he cover up for his dad if I found something incriminating? I went over our conversations, trying to remember what he'd asked and what I'd told him. I even went so far as to wonder if he was the one who pushed me in the subway.

I stopped myself. I was letting my imagination run wild.

When Ryan called, I was back in the East Village. I was tired of pizza, so I'd stopped at a Middle Eastern restaurant. I was perusing the menu, trying to decide what to have.

I didn't bother with preliminaries. "Was your father's name Mike?"

"Yeah, why?"

"A cop named Mike Donovan responded to the call about Georgia Valentine's death. Was that your dad?"

"Yes."

"Why in the hell didn't you tell me?"

"Well, I thought you wouldn't trust me if you knew my father was connected to the case."

"You think? So I trust you more now that you've lied to me?"

"I was planning to tell you. In time. How'd you find out?"

"I'm an investigator, remember? I find out things."

"I should have realized. I'm sorry. Does it make a difference?"

"Of course it does. In fact, your father's actions are suspicious. How can I talk to you about that?"

"Listen, my father and I are two different people. We don't do things the same way. He was old school. He had his prejudices. He did things he shouldn't."

"Like call a death 'suicide' when it was murder?"

"No, he'd never do that. But he hated drugs, and -" He paused to take a breath. "He didn't like blacks. The Irish and blacks have a history of hating each other. He carried that with him."

"But he shouldn't have brought that prejudice to the job."

He sighed. "I know."

We were at an impasse. I didn't know what else to say.

Ryan said. "Believe me when I say, I don't operate that way. I can help you if you'll let me."

"Even if your dad turns out to be culpable?"

"Yes."

This time our conversation had come to an end. I had to think about what he'd said. As a part of the Organized Crime Division, he was invaluable to me. But could I trust him? Did I even like him?

Chapter 35

I FELT GREAT. I'd gone to an aikido dojo in the Chelsea district this morning, paid my twenty dollar mat fee, and had a good workout. It wasn't too far, thirty minutes on the subway with one stop at Union Station.

I'd showered, put on clean clothes, picked up my laptop and was now working at my temporary office, aka Starbucks, looking into Stein and Associates. They had a simple website describing them as a talent and booking agency, giving a phone number and a roster. It included a couple of artists, Vincent "Vinnie" Martino and the Frank Delmonico Quintet.

I couldn't find a website for either one of them, but I found a gig listing. They performed together at Carlo's in the Village three nights a week. Martino was described as an Italian-style crooner and the quartet as a dance band specializing in the music of the Forties and Fifties. It sounded like a place for the old folks to relive their teen years. Not a bad idea.

It was odd that a booking agency had only two clients. Odder still was that they performed at only one venue. I called Stein and Associates and when a woman, probably the nail–filing receptionist, answered, I explained I was Sarah Delaney and interested in booking Vincent Martino for a corporate event. She answered that Mr. Martino was fully booked and not available.

Then I said, "What about the Delmonico dance band. I saw them the other night and liked them."

"The Delmonico band is fully booked also and not available."

"Can you tell me when they would be available? Our event is several months down the road."

"They are booked indefinitely and not available in the near future. Thank you." And she hung up.

Any artist loved to have a regular gig, but it wouldn't leave too much for their managers to do, just collect the money from the venue, take their commission and pay the talent. Pretty cushy. But with only two clients, how could they afford an office and a receptionist? Only if their clients were demanding very high fees.

I put a call into John Beasley. He wasn't home, but I got Bernice.

"Hi, how are you? What's up?" She sounded glad to hear from me.

"Well, quite a lot. I met your favorite person, Maurice LeBlanc."

She groaned. I described my meeting with him and told her he seemed to have dementia.

"I'm sorry to hear anyone has health problems, but I can't feel too sorry for him, the way he treated Georgie."

"But, Bernice, I don't think he's the one who, you know." I didn't want to mention *murder* in a public place, even though my voice wasn't loud.

"No? Why not?"

"Because according to his son, Maurice never had any money. I have the feeling he didn't get the royalty payouts. I think Stein got them."

"Well, that doesn't surprise me. That's what John says he did."

I jumped in. "I wanted to ask John about two acts Stein is managing, Vincent Martino and the Frank Delmonico band. Have you heard of them? Or of Carlo's?"

She gave out a short laugh. "Never heard of the acts, but I know Carlo's."

"What's it like, pretty plush?"

"Heck, no, it's old fashioned, been around forever. Attracts older Italians. And I heard it's a hangout for gangsters. Why are you asking?"

"I wanted to know what those acts are paid for three nights a week."

"Well, all my life I've heard John talk about how musicians are underpaid. I would say two to three hundred a night for the singer, if he's lucky. And less for the musicians."

I let this sink in. "Hmm. That's not a lot, is it?"

"No, but John would be very happy with a steady gig like that. Did you want him to call you?"

"No, thanks. You told me what I wanted to know."

"What about Georgie? Do you know anything yet?"

"I'm getting close. I'll let you guys know as soon as I do, okay?"

We chatted a bit more and rang off.

I got another cup of coffee and sat there thinking about Stein and their clients. I pulled out my pen and notebook. If, say, Martino made three hundred a night and the quintet, say, six hundred, that's nine hundred, a lot to pay out for a small club. But maybe they charged a big cover.

That would be, at twenty percent commission, one eighty a night for Stein. Three nights a week makes twelve nights per month, or a couple of grand a month. Is that enough to pay for an office and a receptionist, not to mention a profit for the owners? I didn't think so. Something else was going on.

I heard my cell phone buzz and checked the caller ID. It was Ryan. It wouldn't be very smart to blow him off. He was my inside man at the NYPD, no matter how much he lied to me.

"Hey, how you doin'?" I tried to be cheerful.

"Still talking to me?"

I ignored that question and told him what I'd found out about Stein and their clients.

He paused a moment before he answered. "You know what it sounds like? It sounds like your first instincts were right, the family is using the place as a laundry."

"What do you mean?"

"To launder money. As a place to funnel their ill-gotten gains, give their income legitimacy."

"So how would it work?"

"They inflate their costs. On the books, they pay those guys a couple of thousand a night, and do the same for all their other expenses. They probably own Carlo's and have other businesses associated with it, a real laundry, for example. They exaggerate their income and costs to explain the money they make illegally."

"I see." I went through it in my mind. It was clever, I had to admit. "Do you know the club? A friend of mine said it was a hangout for Italians."

He laughed. "Not all Italians are in the mafia, but it may be owned by one of the families. I'll see if I can find out."

"I'm thinking of going there tonight."

"After what happened? Are you kidding?"

"No, I'm not going to let that incident stop me. I'm being very careful."

"But a woman alone, with a hit man after her? Is that smart?"

I bristled a little. "I can protect myself. I'm a black belt in aikido." I didn't usually tell people that, but he'd annoyed me with that "woman alone" bit.

I was amused to hear the surprise in his voice. "What? A black belt in martial arts?" He paused. "I'm impressed. You've gotta be the most interesting woman I've met in a long time."

I blushed, even though I was on the phone and he couldn't see me.

Chapter 36

RYAN WAS GOING with me to Carlo's, as a companion not a bodyguard, I made that clear. He had an interest in mob activities, he said, so I agreed. And, besides, I really did want someone to go with me.

He preferred to take a cab rather than his car, so he picked me up in front of the pizza joint next to my building. The restaurant was only a fifteen minute ride, New York cabbie style.

Carlo's was right out of "The Godfather." It looked like the place where Al Pacino shot the mob boss. Dark wood everywhere, white tablecloths, light yellow walls decorated with water colors of Italian scenes, it was intimate and tasteful. Booths lined the right side of the dining room with tables filling the center. The bar was on the right, made of dark wood with shelves of liquor bottles and shiny glasses.

Straight ahead was a stage, which at the moment held a quartet playing what could loosely be termed Italian music, mainly songs recorded by Frank Sinatra, Dean Martin and Tony Bennett. I supposed the singer was on a break.

The place was pretty full for a week night, the tables occupied mostly by older couples, in two and foursomes.

I suppose they could be Italian. They were mostly grey-haired.

A group of men were at the bar, some seated and the others grouped around them. I don't really believe in stereotypes, but I had to say these guys looked like gangsters, at least the ones you see in the movies. They were heavy-set, wore dark suits, had dark hair, and strong features. No cigars, though. They had no compunction about breaking laws, but they seemed to be adhering to the one about no smoking.

The dark-suited host led us to a table where we had a good view of the stage and left us with menus. Ryan ordered a bottle of red wine. We talked about what to order from what seemed to be an interminable list of choices. I finally decided on a fancy-sounding pasta dish preceded by a Caesar salad. Ryan ordered a steak.

Our orders taken, we stared at each other a moment. Ryan said. "I found out about the mob connection with Morey Stein, the Valente family. You were right. They did set him up in business. When the Feds investigated Morey, they indicted him for tax evasion, nothing else. The mob was untouched."

He continued. "After Valente died, the family was taken over by Gianni 'Slim' Farone, who, guess what, owns this place. So we were right, the Stein agency probably launders money for the Valente mob. 'Course they have several other businesses as well. I heard they were also into gambling."

I frowned. "Jesus. So Farone may have ordered one of his goons to off Georgia 'cause she was threatening to accuse Stein of skimming her gig money, which may have led them to the family. As it was, Stein was the only one indicted, wasn't he?"

Ryan said. "Yeah. You may be right. So maybe the Valentes were responsible for the subway attack to keep you from uncovering the money laundering scheme."

"If you know what they're doing, how come you guys haven't arrested them?"

He laughed. "It's not as easy as that. Maybe we know what's going on, but it's hard to prove. They probably have a good accountant who makes the books look right."

The waiter brought a plate of antipasto, salads, and a basket of sour dough, causing my mouth to water. We dug in, not talking.

After we'd finished eating and talking about how good the food was, we ordered espresso. I said. "Tell me about your father."

Ryan looked off into space. "He was a good cop, but he had strong feelings about certain things. Like I told you, he hated drugs, thought they ruined people's lives. He was tough on anyone who took or sold them, especially smack. And he didn't like blacks. Blacks and Irish have clashed for years, with a lot of violence between them. Back in the Twenties my grandfather was beaten by a black gang who accused him of trying to take their job. But -" He gave me an intense look. "- he was a cop first and foremost. He'd never subvert the law. He may have made some bad judgment calls, but he'd never lie or falsify evidence. I'd stake my life on that."

I took a sip of coffee while I thought that over. "So, you're saying he could have jumped to the conclusion Georgia pulled out her IV and administered the drugs herself even though she'd been sedated?"

He met my gaze. "Yes."

I was silent a moment. "Okay, I can buy that. But that doesn't mean he was right."

"Yes, true. Someone else could have administered the drug. And he could have made the wrong assumption. You can't blame him too much. She was known to be an addict."

"And she was black."

He looked down at his coffee cup. "Yes."

"Okay, so who did it? A guy sent by the Valente family?"

"Maybe. But you also suspect the FNA, don't you?"

"Yes, Oblenger was definitely afraid he'd lose his job after that search. Having her die of a drug overdose took the heat off him."

He frowned. "But murdering her to keep a job is pretty radical, isn't it?"

"Yeah, but the man was obsessed with power. Besides, he didn't need to do it himself. He could have had someone do it, in exchange for not being arrested, for example."

"That's true."

I sighed. "I don't know how the hell I'm going to find out who actually did it. But I know she was murdered."

"How can you be so sure?"

Since he'd explained about his father to my satisfaction, I felt I could trust him. I told him about Donna, making him promise to keep quiet.

"Christ. That's evidence enough to bring an indictment if you had a name."

"I know, but I promised I'd never tell anyone and I intend to keep my word."

"Good for you, but how can you complete the investigation? How can you clear Georgia's name?"

I looked at him a moment, wondering if I should tell him my plan. As a cop, he wouldn't like it. But, what the hell, what could he do?

"I've given that a lot of thought. I can tell the story of how she was murdered without using names. I would have it printed in *JazzBeat* magazine. I know the editor, and I know a writer who would do it. That would show the world Georgia Valentine went out as a great artist who had beaten drugs, and not succumbed to them like people think. That's all my client wants."

His eyes met mine. "Okay, then I know what we can do."

Chapter 37

I NOTICED HE was saying "we," as though we were partners. But that was okay. If he could help me solve this crime, I didn't care. It was good to have someone to talk to about it. I enjoyed having a side-kick.

"What?"

"Do you trust me?" He gave me an intense look.

"Yes."

"Okay, just go along with me, no matter what I say or do."

I didn't know what he intended, but he had more experience dealing with these guys than I did, so he was a good partner for this caper.

He gestured to our waiter. When he came to our table, Ryan gave him a card and said. "Take this to your boss, and I don't mean your manager. I mean the big boss. Tell him I'd like to have a friendly chat with him."

The waiter looked at the card, then at Ryan, and turned on his heel. I expected him to go over to the group of men at the bar, but he went through a door at the back of the club.

I stared at Ryan. "What are you gonna do?"

He smiled. "I'm gonna make him an offer he can't refuse."

Where had I heard that before?

Ryan told me more about his father, what a good man he was, and how much he admired him. His mother died when Ryan was young, so the family moved in with his father's parents. They'd lived in the South Ward, which was where the Irish had settled.

I told him the basic details of my life, growing up in a small town in Minnesota and coming to California a few years after high school.

"What made you want to be in law enforcement?"

I shrugged. "I've asked myself that a million times. I think it's because I've always had the urge to set things right. And injustice has always bugged me. I used to get in trouble as a kid because I would call out the teacher when I thought she wasn't being fair."

"I know what you mean. I've had the same urge myself. But have you found it satisfying? Have you set things right?"

Interesting question. I had to think about it a moment. "Well, sometimes I have. Most of my job is doing background checks, which isn't all that satisfying, but the big cases, like homicides or rapes, have a payoff."

"What's an example?"

Before I had a chance to answer, our waiter came back. "Mr. Farone would like to speak with you. Would you follow me, please?"

I gave Ryan a quick glance, but he didn't show any hesitation. He rose and I followed suit. The waiter led us to the door at the back of the room. We walked down a short hallway and then up a flight of stairs to another hall. As we followed our guide, we passed several doors. I glanced into the open ones to see what I guessed were private dining rooms, with tables set for ten or twelve. I turned toward Ryan and he made a card-dealing gesture. So that's where people gambled and that's how Farone made his money.

At the end of the hall was a door labeled PRIVATE with a peep hole at eye level. The waiter knocked and left us. The door was opened by a tall, muscular man with a shaved head and stern features. Wordlessly, he looked us over and stepped aside for us to enter. A slender man in his, I'd guess, early fifties, wearing a pin-striped suit, starched white shirt and red and yellow tie with matching pocket handkerchief, stood by his desk.

160

"Ryan Donovan. I presume." He smiled and held out his hand. His gaze rested on me, his smile broadening. "And friend." He oozed elegance and charm.

"Come in, come in. Have a seat." The muscle man took his place in a corner, his arms crossed over his chest, his eyes watchful. The office was as elegantly furnished as its owner was dressed, a black leather couch and chairs, mahogany desk with matching sideboard, oil paintings on the mustard-colored walls.

We sat on the couch and looked at Farone expectantly. He smiled. "May I offer you a brandy?"

Of course, I had visions of our being drugged and taken for the proverbial "ride," our bodies dumped where no one would ever find them, but Ryan seemed cool.

"That would be nice." He turned his head toward me. "Casey?"

I smiled, hiding my trepidation. "Sure."

Farone went over to the sideboard, poured brandies for the three of us and settled in the chair opposite.

He looked at us directly, smiling. "Now what is it you want to talk to me about?"

Ryan answered. "I'll get right to the point, Mr. Farone. I need a favor and I'm prepared to offer you something in return."

I glanced at him, wondering what the hell he meant. But I'd promised to go along with him, so I kept my mouth shut.

Farone nodded. "I'm intrigued. Please explain, Mr. Donovan."

"I know about your operation here, your connection with Stein and Associates, and the whole thing."

Farone started to demure, but Ryan held up his hand. "Hear me out. I don't need to take it anywhere if you will help me get the information I seek." He halted, his eyes on Farone.

I understood where Ryan was going. He had a helluva lot of nerve, and I began to see him in a new light.

"What information?"

Ryan took a deep breath. "I want to know who gave Georgia Valentine a fatal dose of heroin in her hospital room on May 17, 1963."

Farone's jaw dropped. He was obviously not expecting this. He sat still a moment, staring at Ryan. Then he said. "You mean the jazz singer? Man, that was over fifty years ago. You couldn't expect me to get information on something that long ago."

Ryan smiled. "But, Mr. Farone, I do expect you to get it. And I think you can. I have great faith in you."

Farone laughed. "You're crazy."

Ryan took a sip of his brandy, cool as a cucumber. "Maybe. But I'll expect an answer from you, let's say, tomorrow evening."

"And what if I can't get it?"

Ryan smiled. "Let's not be pessimistic, shall we? I know you can do it." He glanced at me. "And another thing, Mr. Farone, my friend here, who's visiting from San Francisco, had an unfortunate accident the other day. Someone pushed her into the subway rails. Were it not for a good Samaritan who caught her in time, she would be -" Ryan made a face.

Farone's face registered surprise, almost shock. "Surely, Mr. Donovan, you don't think I would do such a thing."

"No, no, of course not. But she had been to the Stein Agency office asking questions and maybe someone there -" Ryan left his sentence unfinished.

Farone pressed his lips into a thin line. "I will look into it."

He directed his next remark to me. "Allow me, Ms. McKie, to apologize on behalf of our city. That is no way to treat a visitor."

We chatted some about the relative virtues of New York and San Francisco, Farone expressing his admiration for North Beach, our Italian district. When I told him I lived only a block or two from there, he smiled his approval. His final gesture was to pick up our check.

Chapter 38

As soon as I woke, I thought about what had gone down with Farone. I couldn't get over how Ryan had handled himself. He was cool, whereas I was apprehensive. And I was more than surprised he would make a deal with a mob boss. We'd talked about it on the way home and he said he didn't mind letting them go for now. They'd get caught sooner or later. And it wasn't as though they were harming anyone but the IRS. I had to laugh to hear a cop say that.

I was inching closer to solving the case, but I wasn't so naïve to think Farone would come up with the killer's name and that would be the end of it. If the Valente family didn't do it, then I was back to square one. I couldn't drop the ball on Oblenger or Maurice Le Blanc. I'd speak with Jack Egan again, see if I could get him to talk about Oblenger's involvement in Georgia's death.

After having my usual breakfast and checking my emails, I called Jack Egan. This time I got him, not his wife. I told him I needed to talk to him again, and he agreed to meet me in the same place, the Chelsea Brewery, at three, after his golf practice. I got the impression I was a welcome diversion from his routine.

I sat there thinking about my next step. I needed to do more checking on the LeBlancs. Jayvon said his father didn't have money, but maybe Jayvon was reaping the benefits of Georgia's talent, collecting her royalties and buying himself fine cars and designer clothes. I had to find out exactly who was Georgia's heir, and if she even had an estate.

That involved wills and contracts, papers that would probably be in the Katz Collection. I called M.K. to see if I could go see her again.

I checked the time, eleven. I figured I could get over there, see her, and then go from there to meet Egan. One thing about this case, I was learning my way around this city.

By the time I dropped my laptop back at the apartment and rode the subway, I arrived at the Katz building at noon. I'd forgotten about eating. I called M.K. and asked her if she wanted me to bring something up to her office. She sounded pleased with the idea and suggested a pita place nearby. I went over there, a place about the size of a large closet and picked up a couple of pita sandwiches.

A few minutes later, M.K. and I were enjoying our lunch in the conference room. I asked her how the collection was coming along.

"Mine or Joseph Katz's?"

"Yours."

She smiled broadly. "Great. I got a bunch of bootleg Sarah Vaughan from a collector. Some of them have really good sound. It's amazing the sound quality you can get from a recorder hidden on your lap." She laughed.

"So you like Sarah?"

"Oh, sure, her and Carmen and Ella, Anita, Dinah. They knew how to sing in those days."

"Are you one of those people who think jazz ended in the Sixties?"

"She smiled." I don't think about stuff like that. There's enough music from the heyday of jazz to last me a lifetime. I won't run out of things to listen to."

I laughed. "I guess not, if you keep adding to your collection. But what happens when you've collected all there is?"

"That'll never happen." She knocked on the table top. "What are you looking for?"

"Well, I want to know if Maurice Leblanc really did get Georgia's royalties and, if he did, how much it amounted to."

"That would mean contracts. I'm sure we have them. We acquired all of Georgia's personal papers. Let me go upstairs and see what I can find. They are in reasonable order, so it shouldn't take me too long. Another cup of tea?"

"Please." She got me another tea and left. I sat there going over what I knew and what I didn't. I knew Oblenger carried out the search of Georgia's hospital room hoping to make an impressive bust, but it backfired. No drugs were found and people were outraged over the invasion of privacy.

Someone telephoned Donna Pellitano, the night nurse, asking her to leave her station, giving the culprit time to go into Georgia's room and administer the overdose. The NYPD, headed by Mike Donovan, ruled that Georgia had self-administered the drugs and did not investigate it as a suspicious death. This was due to Donovan's bias rather than a cover up to a homicide. The hit sounded like the work of a professional, but I didn't know who gave the order, the Valente family, Frederick Oblenger or Maurice Leblanc.

M.K. returned with a bulging file. "Here are her contracts."

She sat opposite me, took a handful of papers from the file and handed it to me. Then she began to read through the remaining contracts.

"Here we go again." She said.

I smiled. "Yeah, ain't we got fun?"

She logged onto a radio station, so we listened to jazz recordings while we worked. It was actually quite pleasant.

After skimming through several contracts, I said. "Looks like Stein screwed her good. All these contracts make him the recipient of future royalties. She gets a fee for the session but nothing else."

M.K. groaned. "Yeah, same thing here. He really took advantage of her. She was probably so happy to get the advances, she didn't worry about what was due her down the line."

"That means he had nothing to fear from her so-called threat."

"Right. She couldn't claim he was cheating her. She signed the contracts."

I sighed. "She should have changed managers."

M.K. shrugged. "I wonder if she even thought of that. She wasn't the only one to work with Morey Stein."

"Why did they stick with him when they knew he was a crook?"

"Because he got the good gigs and he took care of them in other ways. If you got into trouble, you could always call Morey and he'd bail you out."

"Well, that's something, I suppose."

"That's typical of those days. Now it's different. The corporations have taken over. You get your royalties all right, but no one watches your back. It's all impersonal."

I sighed. "I wonder which is better."

M. K. gathered up the contracts and put them back in the file.

I got to the Chelsea Brewery a little early. I took a seat at the bar and ordered the same beer as last time. I wondered how I'd approach Egan. The only thing to do was to ask him outright if Oblenger sent someone to off Georgia. He had no reason to lie to me. He hated the guy.

I sensed him before I saw him. He slid on the stool next to me. "Liked that beer, eh?"

"It's the best beer I ever had."

He laughed. "You're easy to please."

"Maybe as far as beer goes." I shot back.

"Touché." He smiled and gestured to the barkeep for a beer, using bar sign language.

"How's the golf game?"

"I dunno if this is helping or not. I just like it, something to do." He took a sip of beer. "So whatcha got?"

"Well, I've got some pretty solid evidence someone came into Georgia's room the morning she died, someone who didn't belong there."

166

He knew better than to ask my sources. "No shit. Girl, you're good. The cops didn't find diddly squat."

"I heard they didn't look so hard."

"So what are you thinking?"

I met his gaze. "It looks to me like it was a professional hit, but I don't know who ordered it. I'm wondering if it was your boss."

"Oblenger?"

"Yeah, not your wife."

He laughed. "We've talked about that possibility before."

"I know but this time I'm asking you to consider it seriously."

His expression turned grave. "Okay, what would be his motive?"

"To keep his job. You said JFK was thinking of dumping him. The publicity over the Valentine search was bad for him."

He was silent a moment. I could almost hear his mind working.

"Okay, if he really wanted to neutralize that, all he had to do was plant drugs in her room and bust her."

"Why do you suppose he didn't do that?"

"I'll tell you. Oblenger was an asshole, but he was an honest asshole. In fact, he was annoyingly straight, humorless and uptight. He was the kind of guy who insisted on separate checks to make sure everyone paid his fair share. His expense account was as clean as a baby's ass. He might let an addict go, but only if he got good information in return. He had one objective in life, to rid the world of drugs. That's what he lived for. But he was an eagle scout. He'd never arrange a hit, even on the worst kind of addict or pusher. I'm sorry. I wish I could say he done it."

"Jesus, he must have been hell to work for."

"You got that right. He was a man obsessed."

"I wonder how he got that way."

Egan took a swallow of beer. "He used to tell us this story. His mother became addicted to opium after it was prescribed to her for pain relief. When she was coming down from the drug, she'd get sick and send him to the drug store to buy it for her. It wasn't illegal in those days. He watched as she took it and saw the immediate relief it gave her. You'd think this would make him think positive about it, but all he remembered was how sick she was before she took it. He was about nine or ten then, but he never forgot it. He told us that story a bazillion times."

I imagined what it must have done to Oblenger's psyche seeing his mother dependent on drugs. It's no wonder he hated them.

"Well, okay, so I guess I have to rule him out."

"I think you'll have to. You got more suspects?"

I didn't know if I did or not. Stein, Maurice and now Oblenger were off the list. Who was left?

"I'll find some."

He laughed again. "Now who's obsessive?"

When I got back to my neighborhood, I didn't feel like going to the pizza joint again. I wanted some Chinese food and remembered I'd seen a restaurant called the Red Lantern down a few blocks. I felt a sharp yearning to be home, where Chinese restaurants are a dime a dozen, and where I had my good friends Dee and Harry.

I walked to the Red Lantern and took a seat at a small table near the window. After I ordered, I put in a call to Dee.

"Hello." Her deep voice was music to my ears.

"How you doin'? How's your new kitchen?"

She sounded cheerful. "Almost done, thank the Lord. A few more days and I can open. Just in time, too. I'm going broke."

"How do you like it?"

"It's beautiful. Sparkling clean. That motherfucker of an inspector can't complain this time. How's the case?"

"Well, it is moving along, but how it will end, I don't know. My suspect list is getting smaller."

"Oh? How come?"

"A couple of them don't have a good motive."

"Whatcha gonna do?"

"I have another iron in the fire. We'll see. But I'm ready to come home. I'm in a Chinese restaurant now, and the food's not as good as home. And I miss the club."

"We miss you. Harry's always asking me when you're coming back."

We chatted some more, Dee describing the new kitchen in detail. She sounded excited about it. I didn't tell her about Ryan or my brush with the NY subway system. That could wait until I got home. Which I hoped would be soon.

Chapter 39

I'D LIKE TO have a dollar for every middle-aged man who thinks he can sing like Sinatra. Go to any piano bar that lets patrons take the mike and you'll hear one of these bozos making an ass of himself.

Vincent Martino wasn't at a piano bar. He was on stage fronting a quartet doing his best to play the part of Ol' Blue Eyes. Like my friend Dee Jefferson says, people don't realize singing is more than reproducing a melody with your vocal chords. It boils down to two things, time and feeling. If a singer doesn't know how to deal with rhythm, forget it. And if he or she can't tap into the emotions of a lyric, don't bother. Dee won't watch those so-called talent shows because the contestants are so bad.

She would probably tolerate Martino, though. The quartet kept him swinging through Sinatra's signature songs like "Fly Me To The Moon" and "I've Got You Under My Skin." He had a decent baritone and did justice to the lyrics. But he was no Sinatra.

Ryan and I were at Carlo's having dinner, our meeting with Farone scheduled for ten o'clock. It was nice. The food was good, and I was enjoying the music. But I was also feeling a bit apprehensive about our meeting. Who knows how it would turn out?

I said to Ryan. "Do you think Farone will give us an answer?"

He shrugged. "I think he might. These families are a tight community. Even if they're enemies, they know what each other is doing.

They know more about organized crime than our department would ever hope to."

"But don't they take a vow not to rat on anyone?"

"Yes, that's the worst thing a wise guy can do. And if he does, he pays for it."

I made the shape of a gun and pointed it at him.

"Yes, that's the standard punishment."

"So what makes you think Farone will tell you anything?"

"Because he's the capo, the head of the organization. He does what he wants."

"I see." The waiter brought our entrees and we dug in.

I asked Ryan. "How's your veal?"

"Great." Ryan mumbled through a mouth full of veal scaloppini.

We ate our dinner fast, commenting occasionally on the food and the music, but nothing about the case or our personal lives.

A few minutes before ten, the maitre d' came over and politely reminded us of our appointment. As if we could forget. He escorted us to the upstairs office and again the big man with the shaved head answered the door. Farone greeted us warmly and asked if we wanted a drink. Brandy seemed to be his drink of choice and that was okay by me.

Ryan and I sat on the couch and Farone in a chair facing us. He leaned toward me. "Your subway incident had been resolved. The person who confronted you is on his way to Sicily and won't return, and the manager of Stein and Associates, Mr. Rosen, has been transferred to our Florida casino. It will take him a long time before he will be trusted in a position of authority again." He took a sip of brandy. "I apologize on behalf of my organization. I assure you nothing like this will ever happen to you again, not while I'm in charge."

I couldn't say anything. I wasn't used to mob bosses apologizing for trying to kill me, but Ryan was cool, offering his thanks.

Farone continued. "As for the other matter, the death of the singer, we had nothing to do with it. However, I have a few friends inside, and the residents like to talk. They got nothing else to do." He laughed. "So one of my friends overheard a resident tell a story about how he drove someone to the hospital for a hit job. Bottom line is I have a name for you." He paused for effect.

My gaze was riveted on him. I couldn't believe he was about to give us the name of the man who killed Georgia Valentine.

He took a sip of his brandy and continued. "Little Boy Barnacci. He was the driver. He was only eighteen at the time. Now he's an old man who likes to brag about his exploits. But he won't give names. He knows better than that." He paused and gave us a pointed look. "I hope this will satisfy you. It is the best I can do, and I guarantee the information is correct."

"How do you know?" Ryan asked.

"Because Barnacci wants to continue to live to tell his stories. My friends have informed him of what would happen should his information prove to be inaccurate."

Jesus. The cold way Farone smiled gave me the creeps.

Ryan smiled back at him. You'd think they were arranging a golf date. "Thank you, Mr. Farone. I need to talk to him. Will that be all right?"

Farone replied. "If you want him to name the doer, you'll have to make him an offer. He wants to get out. But I would suggest you do it somewhere else. If the residents see him talking to you, he won't live long."

Ryan nodded. "I understand. Where is he?"

"Attica."

"One more thing, Mr. Farone. You realize someone may learn about your operation. Believe me when I tell you they won't hear it from me. You have my word."

They shook hands. As before, we chatted some more, this time about life in New York City, Farone telling us about how he liked to get away to his farm upstate.

In the taxi home, Ryan and I talked about what Farone had told us.

I asked. "Do you believe him?"

"Yes, I do. He had no reason to lie. If Barnacci tells us who he drove to the hospital, we may just have enough evidence to prove Georgia was murdered."

"But remember what Farone said about interrogating him at Attica."

"We won't talk to him there. I'll bring him in on some pretense."

"Aren't you taking a chance making a deal with Farone?"

"How do you mean?"

"Well, I can't imagine your boss would appreciate it."

"Probably not. But Farone will get caught one day."

"But why are you taking such a risk?"

He turned to look at me. "I'll tell you why. I didn't want to mention if before because it sounds so, well, childish. It's because of my grandmother."

"Your grandmother? How so?"

"Well, she loved Georgia Valentine, played her records all the time. She used to say that's what kept her sane. It was her way of escaping life with a cop husband and son and us bratty kids."

"I can understand that. Going to hear my friend Dee sing does the same for me."

"Anyway, my grandmother hated it that Georgia died of a drug overdose. She thought it destroyed the mystique."

"That's how my clients feel."

"I know."

I was taken back. "Does your grandmother live in New York?"

"Ryan smiled." No, she's gone now, but I do this for her anyway."

I gave Ryan a long look. He was a pretty nice guy. For a cop.

Chapter 40

I AWOKE WITH a feeling of anticipation, like a kid on Christmas morning. Ryan and I were interviewing Little Boy Barnacci today. If he gives us the name of Georgia's killer, my case will be solved. Of course, I couldn't bring anyone to trial. I'd promised not to involve Donna. Also Barnacci wouldn't agree to testify or he'd be signing his death warrant.

But that didn't matter. What was important was the knowledge that the great jazz singer Georgia Valentine hadn't given herself a fatal injection of heroin, either accidentally or deliberately. Her legend as one of the world's greatest jazz singers will survive. She'd be taken off the list of artists who died of a drug overdose.

Ryan had arranged for Barnacci to be brought to One Police Plaza on a pretext that he was being re-interviewed regarding a gang killing. He was to be treated as a hostile witness, as least at the prison, so the inmates wouldn't suspect him of snitching.

I would sit in on the interview, but Ryan would do the questioning. I was supposed to meet him at his office at eleven. I just had time to do my morning walk, which I had instituted a few days ago, and check my emails. I walked down 3ʳᵈ for several blocks, turned right, went down a block and walked back. It was a far cry from my favorite walk at home where I walk to Crissy Field along the Bay with the Golden Gate Bridge in bas relief against the deep blue water. But the people watching made up for the lack of a view.

When I returned, I had a quick shower, dressed, and took my laptop over to Starbucks. My email box was filled with the usual pleas for political donations, which, if I honored, would put me in the poorhouse.

The whole concept of spending money to get elected was crazy. Radio and television stations should provide candidates with air time to present their ideas. Now it's a matter of which candidate amasses the most money to defeat his opponent. Most of the money goes for ads, which are either negative or filled with lies. That's no way to elect leaders that literally rule the world.

But among the solicitations was an email from Harry. What was up? Harry never emailed me. Maybe he missed me. I opened it and read:

I hate to bother you when you're on a case, but I'm worried about Dee.
My pulse started racing. Was Dee sick?
The remodel is finished and she had another
inspection, but failed again. The club is still closed and Dee is depressed
and not herself. Is there anything you can do?
Harry

What the hell? Why wouldn't a brand new kitchen pass inspection? Something is wrong. I took a sip of coffee. My mind went through a list of scenarios.

Did someone have it in for Dee? That wasn't likely. She was highly respected for running a good club, one that helped bring business into North Beach. Was it racial prejudice? That would be hard to believe, since she'd been there since the Seventies with no problems.

My mind whipped through the possibilities. She had a very desirable location in one of the most popular tourist districts in the City. Maybe it was a scheme orchestrated by someone who wanted to get that spot. It had been done before, especially in North Beach. The problem was they were succeeding. I never knew Dee to be this down.

I wracked my brain. What could I do from three thousand miles away? I couldn't leave now that I was so close to solving the case. I needed help. Harry? No. He was a smart guy, but I needed someone experienced. Like me.

Then it came to me. Nick Dasher. He was a PI I'd worked with a few years ago on a missing person case. He'd asked me to help check out Marin County while he worked the East Bay and the Peninsula. His job was to find a fifteen-year-old girl who'd gone missing. He was under a time crunch because her very wealthy parents figured she'd be killed if we didn't find her fast.

As it turned out, she'd run away with her older boyfriend. I found them in a motel in Stinson Beach. Nick, who got a huge fee for finding her, was extremely grateful.

I found his number and, getting a recording, left a message asking for his help. I told him to call me ASAP. My relief was immediate. I knew he'd call me back and give the problem his full attention.

I replied to Harry not to worry. I was on it. I didn't have to explain further. To know I was working on it would satisfy Harry, who thought I walked on water.

I checked the time. Jesus, I had to hurry. I fast-walked to the subway station and caught the next car. In fifteen minutes, I was walking up the steps of the NYPD building and got to Ryan's office at five to eleven.

I waited fifteen minutes, my anxiety level ratcheting up. What if something went wrong and we won't be able to do the interview? I thumbed through *Bail Bond Digest*, but none of the articles caught my interest.

Ryan came out and I jumped up to greet him. He smiled. "Don't worry. Everything's going according to plan. Come on in."

I followed him down the hall to an interview room.

Before we entered, he said in a low voice. "Let me do the talking. It'll work better if there's only one person asking the questions. If I forget something or you think of something to ask, give me a high sign and we'll leave the room to talk, okay?"

"Sure, whatever you say."

We went in. Barnacci was sitting at a table, his head hanging down. He seemed to be asleep, but he looked up as we entered.

"Barnacci, Ms. McKie here is sitting in, but I'll be asking the questions, okay?"

He mumbled something.

His hair was gray and thin, I could see that he'd been blond. His once boyish face had succumbed to the forces of gravity, giving him a sad look. But his nickname had stuck despite the change of appearance.

"Barnacci, we understand you were once the driver for the Valente family. Isn't that true?"

He mumbled. "Yeah, I guess so. That was a long time ago."

"I know it was. You were only eighteen and you probably got sucked into something you didn't know much about. Would you agree with that?"

Barnacci met Ryan's gaze. "Somethin' like that."

"You drove them wherever they told you to go, right?"

"Yeah."

"And you waited for them, I suppose."

"Yeah."

"And I don't imagine you knew what they did, did you?"

"Nah, they never tol' me nothin'."

"Did they talk in the car? Did you ever get any idea what they did?"

"Nah, they din't talk."

"I see, but I bet you remember some of the places you took them."

"Maybe."

"'Specially if something came down at the same time and place."

Barnacci looked up sharply. "Could be."

Ryan sighed. "Let's talk about the night Georgia Valentine died."

Barnacci's expression changed. His facial muscles tightened and he took on a wary look.

When he didn't respond, Ryan continued. "You know who she was, don't you, Barnacci?"

"Yeah, a singer. Popular."

"They said she died of an overdose of heroin, did you hear that?"

Barnacci got more tense. "Yeah, I heard somethin' about it."

"It was May 17, 1963. Were you driving for the Valentes then?"

Barnacci looked from Ryan to me and back again.

"Might have been, don't remember."

Ryan's voice rose. "Don't give me that bullshit, Barnacci. You know goddamned well you were driving for them then. You told everyone at Attica about it."

Barnacci stared at Ryan, his lips beginning to quiver. He practically whispered. "Maybe I did, but I din't know what they were doin'. I swear. I just drove."

Ryan's voice softened. "That's no excuse. A driver can be indicted if a murder is involved, you know that, don't you?"

"I guess so."

Ryan got loud again "You know goddamned well it does. Don't play innocent. You're better off being straight with me."

Barnacci perked up. "Whaddya mean?"

Ryan leaned closer to Barnacci. "I mean if you tell me the truth, I can fix it so you don't get indicted. And if you don't, you're screwed, one way or another."

Barnacci sneered. "Makes no difference. I'm in for life."

Ryan leaned back in his chair and crossed his arms.

"You come up for parole, don't you?"

Barnacci's gaze was fixed on Ryan. "Yeah."

"Well, maybe I can put in a word for you and help you with the parole board."

"You could do that?"

"Yes."

"If I tell you about that night?"

"Yes."

"You swear?"

"Yes."

Barnacci sat there for a few minutes, not speaking, staring at Ryan.

"How do I know I can trust you?"

"You don't, but it's the only chance you've got to get out of Attica."

Barnacci sat still for a full five minutes before he spoke.

"Okay, uh, I picked up the passenger at the usual place, a pizza joint in Queens. Uh, it was close to midnight. I don't remember exactly. Drove to the hospital, uh, parked near the emergency entrance. The passenger got out, told me to wait about twenty minutes, which I did. It was fine, no one bothered me. I smoked a couple of cigarettes and waited, uh, like I was told. Then the passenger came out, got in the car, and I drove back to the pick-up spot, the, uh, pizza place. The passenger got out and went in. I drove home. I didn't know nothin' about, uh, what went down. The next day I heard that singer died. That's all."

I was riveted, listening to the story, my senses taut.

Ryan kept his eyes on Barnacci, staying quiet.

Then he asked the million-dollar question. "Who was the passenger?"

Barnacci looked stricken. "I swear I don't know who it was. It was some nurse."

"A woman?"

"Yeah."

"And she was dressed like a nurse?"

"Yeah."

"What did she look like?"

"I didn't see her that good. It was dark and I knew better than to give her the eye, you know."

"Yes, I know. They didn't like that."

"No."

Ryan's voice was soft. "But describe her the best way you can."

"Okay," Barnacci sucked in his breath. "She wasn't young but she wasn't old, neither, know what I mean? She was in between. And I could tell by her voice that she wasn't no broad, know what I mean?"

"Yes, I do."

"As best as I could see, she was pretty, and -" he glanced at me. "- she had a nice body, a nice ass."

We were both silent. Finally, Ryan said. "Anything you can add, Barnacci?"

He met Ryan's eyes. "No, I swear. That's all I know. I don't know nothin' else."

"Did you ever drive the woman again?"

He shook his head. "Nah, never saw her again. Never heard nothin' about her, neither."

"Okay, Barnacci. We'll take you back now. You can tell the guys that we wanted to talk to you about that recent hit. But we got nothing out of you. I'll have the officers rough you up a little just to make it look real. Okay with you?"

Barnacci gulped. "You'll talk to the parole board?"

"Yes, I will. You have my word on that."

Chapter 41

RYAN AND I were sitting on a bench at One Police Plaza eating hot dogs and washing them down with coffee.

"You believe Barnacci?" I asked.

"Yes, I do. He had no reason to lie."

I took a bite of my hot dog, which I had to say was better than the ones I got at home. Among other things, New York had the best hot dogs.

"But would they send a woman on a hit? It doesn't seem likely." I spoke as if I knew all about the mafia, but the truth was all I knew about the mafia was from movies and television. In San Francisco, we had Chinese gangs.

Ryan said. "They don't usually, but if they thought a woman had a better chance of getting into the hospital at night -"

"True. Jesus. Who the hell could it be? This shoots all my theories straight to hell."

Ryan smiled. "I'm sure you'll come up with another idea. Meanwhile, I have to get back to work. You'll be okay here?"

"Sure."

Now that Farone has discovered who'd tried to kill me, I wasn't worried anymore and had abandoned my cap and trench coat. But that didn't prevent Ryan from playing the protector. I could have resented it, but actually I thought it was kinda cute.

I watched him walk away with what I had to admit was a warm feeling. Was I falling for this guy? After I had vowed never to become involved with a cop again? Jesus, what's wrong with me?

Just then my cell phone rang. It was Nick Dasher. I explained what I wanted him to do, investigate the health inspector who was assigned to check out Dee's club.

"See if he has any connections to real estate developers or anyone else with an interest in buying the club."

He accepted the assignment without asking any questions. Why I wanted to know was irrelevant. He'd do what I asked no matter my reasons, knowing I'd do the same for him. PIs had a code of quid pro quo.

Dee's problem off my mind, my thoughts went back to the case. The big question now was discovering the identity of the woman Barnacci drove to the hospital. The question percolated in my brain all the way home.

All my suspects were male. Did one of them send a woman to do the job? Maybe Maurice sent one of his girls. But Barnacci said the woman had class, so that doesn't fit. And I can't imagine Oblenger or Morey sending a woman. Was there a female who hated Georgia? A rival singer? An angry wife?

The only person I could think of to ask was Bernice. It was late afternoon. As soon as I got back to the apartment, I called her. I did the polite chit-chat thing, then asked her what I wanted to know.

"Bernice, did Georgia have any women who disliked her?"

Bernice laughed aloud. "Did she! A couple of other singers resented her, out of envy. She slept with married men, so their wives probably hated her. Want me to go on?"

"I mean REALLY hated her, enough to, you know."

"Give her enough shit to kill her?"

"Yeah, did anyone dislike her that much?"

"Let me think a minute." She paused. I could hear her breathing. "One woman used to come to her hospital room. She'd been Georgia's dealer and she wanted to get her on dope again. But Georgia refused. That made her mad."

"Do you know her name? Can you describe her?"

"White, thin, brown hair, young, not bad looking and a little mannish. In fact, I thought she had a crush on Georgia."

"Was it reciprocal?"

"You mean did Georgia like her back?"

"Yeah, did they have something going on?"

"Nah, I don't think so. All she wanted was Georgie to buy drugs off her. And Georgie wouldn't."

My heart beat faster, as it always did when I was about to get some good intel. "What's her name?"

Silence. "Let me ask John." I heard muffled voices and in a few minutes, Bernice came back. "Sugar Sheldon and she's still around. She owns a bar in Brooklyn, named after her. It's a lesbian hangout. John don't know if she's dealing any more. He said she was a big dealer back in the day. She was tough. If you owed her money and couldn't pay, she could be lethal. His words." She took a deep breath. "Does that help?"

"It sure does. He say anything else?"

"Yeah, be careful."

I laughed. It was hard for me to be afraid of a woman, lesbian or not. Unless she was also a black belt. I guess that makes me a sexist.

Well, I'd been to gay bars lots of times, but never to a lesbian one, so I was in for a new experience.

My phone rang. It was Ryan checking in. I mentioned the new information on the female drug dealer.

"Sugar Sheldon, huh? Haven't heard of her."

"She's a definite suspect. I'm thinking of going to see her tonight."

"Where is she?"

I explained about the lesbian bar.

"I'd offer to come with you," he chuckled, "but I imagine you'd do better on your own."

"I guess. I have no idea what to expect."

He laughed. "You know damn well what to expect, the same thing that happens in any singles bar. You'll get hit on."

"Well, I'm not sure how to react."

"Just as you would with a man, say yes or no. Call me when you're free and we can meet. I want to hear all about it."

I bet he does.

Chapter 42

GETTING TO SUGAR'S was surprisingly easy. I only had to take one subway. From the station, I walked about ten minutes through a neighborhood with brownstones and upscale restaurants. It might be fun to live here, I thought, a feeling that only lasted a moment.

The club was squeezed in between two fairly large buildings, painted a dark blue with black-curtained windows. No neon sign, just the name *Sugar's* painted above the entrance.

I paused at the entry door, took a deep breath and went in. I had to admit I was a little apprehensive, why, I don't know. The first thing I noticed was a pool table. A couple of women were playing while others watched, beer bottles in hand. A bar was on the right, with women perched on stools, a television set over the bar tuned to a basketball game. Just like any other joint.

I decided to check out the whole place before I asked for Sugar, hoping to god she wasn't an absentee owner. Straight ahead was a dance floor surrounded by tables. A small stage sat at the far end of the area, where some scantily-clad women were pole dancing. Now, that was a little weird, but logical, at the same time. The music was recorded, a DJ at the turntables.

It was your typical urban bar with one tiny exception. Everyone in the place was female. As I walked through, several women gave me the once-over, but I kept my eyes straight ahead.

A set of stairs led to the upper floor where I found another bar and dance floor. A back door led to an outdoor patio occupied by several patrons enjoying Sugar's special barbecue. I was surprised by the club's size. It didn't look this large from the outside. And even more surprising, it was full. Sugar seemed to be running a very successful club. I headed for the bar, took a stool and ordered a beer.

I swiveled on the stool to watch the dancers. I was used to seeing women dancing together. They do it all the time. But they don't use dance as foreplay as these women did, dancing close, grinding and kissing. Most of the dancers were young, but I noticed a few older women, not many. Some of the dancers looked straight, but others were mannish in their dress and behavior. After a few minutes, the scene lost its novelty and I turned back to the bar and took a pull from my beer.

I caught the bartender's eye and nodded for her to come over.

"Is Sugar here?"

I held my breath, hoping she wouldn't say something like "Sugar never comes in anymore" or worse, "Sugar's dead."

She answered. "Yeah, she's over there." She tilted her head toward the end of the bar, where I saw an older women looking down at the bar, going over checks, probably.

I thought a moment about what approach to take. I wouldn't get very far if I told her the truth, that I was considering her as a suspect in Georgia Valentine's murder. I'd be better off passing myself off as a journalist, something I did often. It justified asking questions but didn't pose a particular threat.

I picked up my beer and moved down the bar to where Sugar was standing. She looked at me briefly, then back down at her paper work.

"Hi, Sugar. How ya doin'?" My standard opening.

She looked up and actually smiled. "Pretty good. You?"

"I'm great. You have a fantastic club here."

"Thanks. And you are?"

Jesus, had I blown my cover already? "I'm Casey, I'm doing a piece on Georgia Valentine for *JazzBeat* magazine and wanted to ask you a couple of questions."

The smile disappeared, replaced by a frown. "Oh, yeah? What about?"

"Can we go somewhere and talk?"

"We can talk okay here. Whaddya wanna know?" She looked down at the papers.

"You knew her, right?"

"Yeah, so did a lot of people. She was a famous jazz singer or hadn't you heard?"

Oh, oh, hostility. This wasn't gonna be easy. Might as well get to the point. "You used to supply her with drugs, right?"

I thought she was gonna throw me out, but instead she laughed. "What is this, anyway, some kind of joke?"

"No, someone told me you were a dealer and Georgia was one of your customers."

"What if it's true, what's it to you?"

Man, this lady is tough. Bernice had described her as brown haired, young and thin, and fairly attractive. Well, she wasn't any of those things now. She had white hair worn in a buzz cut and a stocky body. She was wearing jeans and a tee-shirt emblazoned with the club's logo. She wore no make-up or jewelry and, if it weren't for the bulges on her chest, she could have passed for a man.

"Sugar, I'm a journalist on an assignment, looking into Georgia Valentine's death. Some people think she didn't overdose voluntarily, but was murdered. I wanted to get your take on it. And I don't give a shit if you sold drugs."

She looked up at me sharply, stared at me a moment. "Okay, let's go over to a booth."

As soon as we were seated, I said. "People told me Georgia was clean when she got out of jail and stayed that way. Is it true? Was she taking drugs when she was in the hospital?"

"No, dammit. I tried to get her to buy off me, but she wouldn't. I gave up trying. I visited her, but as a friend, not a customer. I liked her."

Jesus. I was getting close to the truth now. I believed her. She had no reason to lie. If she had sold Georgia drugs, she could have simply told me to get lost.

"How do you think she got the stuff that killed her?"

She grimaced. "I think someone gave it to her, and I don't think she asked for it."

My pulse was racing. This was the closest I'd been to learning what happened. "Who?"

She gave out a short laugh. "Ah, that's the big question, isn't it?"

"Can you make an educated guess?"

Her eyes narrowed. "You gonna quote me?"

"No. I just want the truth. I'm not out to make trouble for anyone. A lot of people want to know how Georgia really died."

"Well, it coulda been Maurice. He was a sorry excuse for a man. He only hung around Georgia for her money."

"Yeah, but I have a witness who said it was a woman."

She sneered. "And you believed that? Honey, have you ever seen a drag queen? Some of those bitches are hot. Some of them even work the streets, and if the johns can't tell, who could? Maurice could have sent one of them."

"Yeah, but my witness said it was a high class woman in her forties."

Sugar laughed. "You ain't been around much, have you? Some of those bitches put on a good act."

"Do you think a prostitute would have committed murder if Maurice asked them to?"

She rolled her eyes. "If they were strung out and he offered them some shit, they would."

Jesus. This adds a whole new wrinkle in the story. But Sugar is right. Just because Barnacci said it was a woman doesn't mean it was.

Sugar rose from her seat. "Honey, it coulda been lots of people. I really don't know and couldn't even guess. But I'll tell you this. Georgia didn't do it herself. She was clean. I oughtta know. I tried like hell to get her back on the stuff. I'm ashamed of myself now. I really am. But at least I can say I didn't cause her death. That's one thing in my favor. Now I better get back to work. I don't trust nobody else with those checks."

I thanked her and got the hell out of there.

As soon as I was outside, I called Ryan.

He said. "Ready for dinner?"

In New York, people go out at all hours. It wasn't unusual to leave the house at midnight for a night on the town. "Yeah, I'm famished. Got a place in mind?"

"You like Indian?"

"Love it."

"Okay, get inside somewhere and I'll pick you up in twenty minutes."

I spied a wine bar on the corner and went in there. I texted him the address and sat by the window so I could leave as soon as I saw his car.

As I sipped my Pinot Chardonnay, I thought about my interview with Sugar. She'd provided the final testimony. I had no doubt Georgia Valentine had been murdered. But still I felt like I'd gone back to square one. I'd been sure it was a woman who killed Georgia, eliminating Maurice, Stein and Oblenger. Jesus, who the hell was it? And was it a real woman or a man in drag?

My thoughts were floating round my brain like eddies in a stream, not going anywhere. I was close, but I hadn't crossed the finish line. Maybe it was impossible to solve this murder, a depressing thought.

Ryan's car pulled up outside and I hustled out.

He leaned over and opened the door for me. "How was it?"

I slid into the seat. "Interesting, but as you said, just like any bar, except it was all women. They even had pole dancers."

"No shit. That seems odd."

"Well, not when you think about it. Lesbians like women, remember?'

"True. You talk to the owner?"

"Yeah, she said Georgia was clean when she died. She tried to sell her stuff, but Georgia wouldn't go for it. She thinks someone shot her up, but she has no idea who it was."

"No guesses?"

"No, but she brought up a good point. It might have been a man dressed like a woman."

"Of course, that's right. It never occurred to me. It's possible. Someone figured a nurse has a better chance of getting into the hospital without attracting attention. So they have their hit man dress like a woman. Makes a lot of sense."

I didn't answer. I was let down. Even though Sugar had all but proved Georgia hadn't taken the drugs herself, the suspect list was wide open again.

Ryan said. "There it is, Tandoor, the best Indian restaurant this side of Mumbai."

Like most every other restaurant I'd seen in New York, it was on the bottom floor of a multi-storied building, butted up against other establishments and painted a dark color. On one side was a juice bar and the other, a phone store. The rest of the block was, like the city itself, eclectic. I spotted a revivalist storefront church, a large building with curtained windows and no identifying sign. Who knows what went on inside? I also noticed a Chinese restaurant, a tiny park, and a boarded-up building.

The interior of the Tandoor was nicely decorated, painted walls with framed prints. It had a small bar, with the kitchen in a closed space behind it. The place was nearly full, a sign that the food was good. Real Indian music played softly in the background.

We ordered samosa, lamb masala and rice, and an order of naan, Indian baked bread, which I loved. Ryan asked for a bottle of Pinot Noir, which he said goes with Indian food.

As soon as we had our glass in hand, I began to fill him in on my adventures. I described Sugar's and its owner and what she said about not being able to get Georgia to buy dope.

"And you'll be interested to know that no one hit on me. Not a soul."

He laughed. "I hope you're not disappointed."

I just smiled. Actually I was a little insulted.

"Lady, it sounds like you've almost completed the puzzle. You must be happy."

"You're right. I ought to be ecstatic, but I feel as lost as when I started this investigation."

Ryan said. "What about your real nurse, the one who was paid to look the other way? Didn't she say a man called her?"

"Yeah. That fits, doesn't it? Maybe it was a man who killed Georgia, after all."

"But Barnacci said the woman he drove was kinda sexy. Remember what he said?"

"About the nice ass?"

"Yes."

"Well, as Sugar reminded me, some men in drag can look sexy. She's right. I've seen them myself."

"Of course you have. You're from San Francisco."

It annoyed me when people associate San Francisco with gayness. It's true that we have a gay neighborhood, the Castro, but that doesn't mean everyone in the city is gay. But I didn't correct him. I hadn't the energy.

Chapter 43

THE NEXT MORNING, I was still feeling down. I didn't even feel like getting out of bed. I'd spent all this time, and I didn't know who the killer was. I knew Georgia had been murdered, but not by whom.

My cell phone rang. I grabbed it from the nightstand, thinking to myself it was probably more bad news.

It was Bernice. "'There's something I ought to tell you. I should have mentioned it before."

A spurt of adrenaline shot through me.

"Georgie had an affair with a woman, a very wealthy woman."

I sat up, my senses totally alert. "Are you telling me Georgia Valentine was a lesbian?"

"No, no, she just accepted love wherever she found it. And this woman was crazy about her. For a while."

Jesus. I never expected this. "Who was it?"

"Dina Von Rillerbach."

"Von Rillerbach. Aren't they that super wealthy family?"

"Yeah, they make the Rockefellers look like paupers."

"Jesus. Tell me about it."

She sucked in her breath. "Well, Bernice told me when she was in the hospital and thinking about writing a book. The affair happened was when she was working in the Village. Back in the Forties. This beautiful young debutante used to come in with her friends. She got a crush on Georgia and one thing led to another."

"And what happened?"

"Well, Dina's mother took her to Europe. And that was the end of it."

Good god, this sounded like one of those British dramas you see on television. "What did Georgia do?"

"Oh, she didn't care. She went on with her life. She always had her choice of lovers."

"And what happened to the girl?"

"She married a very wealthy man and became one of those society women you read about in the papers."

"Jesus, that's frickin' interesting."

"I have to go. John will be back in a few minutes. And, Casey -"

"Yeah?"

"Please keep this between us, okay?"

"Sure." Unless it becomes important, I added to myself.

I sat there thinking. So Georgia had an affair with a wealthy society girl when she was young. So what? What would that have to do with her murder twenty years later?

I needed to know more about this Dina Von Rillerbach.

I got dressed, grabbed my laptop bag and went over to Starbucks to use their Wi-Fi.

I picked up a cappuccino and went online. I got a bunch of links and started with Wikipedia. I read the lengthy entry.

The Von Rillerbach fortune was made centuries ago in Europe and increased by James, a male heir who emigrated to America at the turn of the century. James invested in shipping and railroads, taking advantage of the burgeoning industrial revolution. His enterprises were fabulously successful, resulting in his branch of the Von Rillerbachs becoming one of the wealthiest families in the world.

I went to other links and, after a few hours, had filled in Dina's story.

Dina was the youngest daughter of James's second wife, Camilla, whose main interests seemed to be her social status, her male conquests, her parties, and her residences. She hadn't time for mothering, so her daughter was raised by a series of nurses and governesses. She lived most of her young years at boarding schools.

Dina's debut party was the highlight of the 1945 social season, making headlines in the leading newspapers and magazines, one of which featured her on its cover.

As a debutante, Dina spent her time going to dinner parties and other social events. Her best friends were two other wealthy and beautiful society girls, the three of them often going "slumming" in Greenwich Village, making the rounds of jazz clubs. People, especially men, were intrigued by this trio of beautiful, rich young women.

I took a sip of cappuccino. This corroborated the story Georgia told Bernice. If Dina had hung out in jazz clubs, she would have seen Georgia perform and probably met her. According to Bernice, Georgia had free and easy ways and might well have turned Dina's admiration into a sexual affair. Such an alliance would be old hat for the jazz singer, but for the young debutante getting her first taste of the world outside the confines of her mansions and boarding schools, it would have been an exciting adventure.

I continued filling in Dina's story.

Dina's trip to Europe with her mother happened in 1946. Half a year later, at the age of twenty, she married her equivalent, a scion of another wealthy family. She dabbled in various ventures, volunteering as a nurse, going to cooking school, taking painting lessons and attempting to write a novel.

Dina's father, James, had long since tired of Camilla's lifestyle and divorced her, effectively cutting her off financially and socially. She had to

*live off Dina, who had a huge trust fund. Maybe to regain her income
and social status, Camilla took up with various wealthy men.*

*Meanwhile, Dina's marriage to the wealthy scion broke up. She married
three more times, the last one to a Reynolds Davis producing a daughter
she named Savoy. Dina lived the same life as her mother, attending and
hosting dinner parties and travelling to Europe, leaving the daughter in
boarding schools or with relatives.*

*Savoy, perhaps in reaction to her mother and grandmother, chose a dif-
ferent path. She pursued a career in the theater, but was no dilettante.
She went to acting school and paid her dues by taking bit parts whenever
she could. In time she became a highly respected actress with a solid career. Although not a household name, she worked steadily, performing
in both on- and off-Broadway. In fact, she was currently appearing in
"Three's a Crowd" at the Beaumont Theater.*

I should talk to her, but what would I say? "Hey, I heard your
mother had a lesbian affair with Georgia Valentine, the jazz singer who
supposedly died of an overdose. Oh, yeah, that was fifty years ago."

But I couldn't ignore the affair even if it had nothing to do with
Georgia's murder.

Chapter 44

I COULDN'T REMEMBER the last time I'd been to the theater. I'd gone to see a mystery play with a friend several years ago. The audience was part of the production and, after we witnessed the crime, a murder, of course, we were supposed to figure out who done it. I saw so many flaws in how they went about solving the mystery, I couldn't enjoy it. I knew at the outset who the culprit was, but kept it to myself. After that experience, I came to the conclusion I preferred to go hear music than watch a play.

But "Three's a Crowd" was no murder mystery. It was about a dysfunctional family - is there any other kind? - who were so screwed up, they all needed psychiatric help. Savoy played the main character's best friend, who was "secretly" in love with her friend's husband, but who listened with great sympathy to her friend's suspicions about her husband's infidelity. I didn't care much for the play, but I thought Savoy did a good job portraying this hypocritical woman.

I told her I would be at the play and hoped she would talk to me afterwards. She said to meet her at the stage door. After the play ended, I fast-trotted to the door, where I saw a couple of young people standing around, holding programs for signing. The lead male actor came out and the autograph seekers crowded around him. Then as the female lead emerged, they moved over to her.

Savoy came out next, looking like she was in a hurry, but no one went up to her with a program. She had a supporting role, so I guess she wasn't autograph material. I approached her and said as quickly as I could. "Miss Davis, I'm the private investigator who called you. I'm wondering if we could talk for a few moments. It's about your mother, Dina Von Rillerbach."

She looked at me, questioning. "My mother?"

"Yes, I wanted to talk to you about her friendship with Georgia Valentine."

"The jazz singer?"

"Yes, I'm investigating her death."

"Didn't that happen years ago?"

"Yes, in 1963, but some new evidence shows she might have been murdered."

"Murdered? What would my mother know about that?"

"I don't know. I'm talking to people who knew her, trying to get at the truth. Maybe you could help me."

She looked at her watch. "Well, just for a minute. I have an evening performance and need some time at home before I have to come back."

I said. "Ten minutes."

She smiled. 'Okay, let's go down the street to the Stage Door, they're quick."

She strode to the small coffee shop with me following. It was one of those holes in the wall where you mostly got stuff to go, but they had a couple of tables in the back.

Savoy went up to the counter, where the brown-skinned man smiled.

"Hello, Miss Davis. Your usual?"

She turned to me. "Black coffee okay?"

I nodded.

"Make it two, Guillermo."

She picked up the two paper cups he set on the counter and brought them to one of the tables.

When we were seated, she took a sip of coffee and then looked at me expectantly.

I felt I had to talk fast or she'd walk out, she was such a quick-moving person.

"First, let me say I thought you were excellent in the play."

She smiled. "Tell me, what would my mother know about Georgia Valentine's death? I know she admired her. She played her records all the time."

"Someone told me that they were friendly at one time, when your mother and her friends spent time in Greenwich Village, when they were young and single."

"And wild." She smiled again. "Yes, I've heard those stories. Mother loved telling us about her days as a debutante."

"Did she mention knowing Georgia?"

"I don't remember if she did. She told us about the movie stars she met and dated, though. I was quite impressed. It was hard to imagine my mother going out with Errol Flynn and Howard Hughes. I thought at first that she was making it up, but it was all true. So she may very well have known Georgia Valentine."

"A friend of Georgia's told me that they were quite close. I understand your mother went to Europe about that time. I'm wondering if the reason was to separate her from Georgia."

Savoy frowned. "It was more a matter of tradition. It was de rigueur then for young people to go on what they called a Grand Tour before settling down to marriage. Besides, why would anyone want to break up a friendship?"

"Well, Georgia was black, a jazz singer, and a drug addict, none of which qualified her as acceptable company for a debutante."

Savoy laughed. "Yes, I imagine Mother's actions were upsetting for the family. Granny could have taken her to Europe to get her away from bad influences. That would be in character. But that was in the Forties. And you say Georgia died in 1963. I don't see the connection."

"Well, I understand your mother was about to be married again, to a prominent man. If he heard about this relationship, it might have messed up the marriage plans."

Savoy frowned. "That's ridiculous. Mother went to jazz clubs when she was young and knew a jazz singer, so what?"

I sucked in my breath. "Because the way I heard it, they were lovers."

Savoy's eyes opened wide and her mouth dropped. "Lovers? Mother and Georgia Valentine?"

"Yes, that's what a good friend of Georgia's told me."

Savoy stood. "I don't believe it. I don't know what you're after, but I won't listen to any more of this. You don't know what you're talking about."

With that, she left.

Well, that went well. But she proved my point. The Von Rillerbachs didn't like bad publicity. I called Bernice and told her what happened. "Are you positive that Dina and Georgia had a sexual affair?"

"Well, I never saw them in the act, but Georgia told me they did, and she didn't have no reason to lie. She was very open about sex. She'd talk about it like someone else would talk about what they had for dinner. Man or woman, it was all the same to her. I was very young then and was kinda shocked about it, but that was the way she was. She was very honest."

"How could I check to see if it was true?"

"Let me see." She paused. "Wait a minute, that gossip columnist. I can't think of his name right now. He wrote about Georgia all the time, I don't know who fed him the gossip, but he seemed to know everything."

"What was his name?"

"It's coming. M-something, Melvin, Melvin Mitchell. He wrote for one of the big papers, can't think of the name."

Joan Merrill

"That's okay, Bernice, I can find it on Google."

"On what?"

"On the Internet."

"Oh, the computer thing. Okay. Good luck."

Chapter 45

I WENT BACK to my apartment and picked up my laptop and went over to Starbucks. I looked up *Melvin Mitchell* and discovered his columns and assorted papers were available on Google, which made me extremely happy. I could sit there on my butt and not have to traipse over to the library and spool through microfilm, one of the most tedious jobs in the world.

I estimated the time period Dina and her friends would have been hanging out at the Village. It would have started after her debut in 1945 and ended before her trip to Europe the following May. I coordinated those dates with Georgia's schedule, which I got from her biography, the official one written in 1985.

Mitchell wrote a daily column, so I had to go through hundreds of issues to find mention of Dina Von Rillerbach. Aside from getting up to get a refill and to go to the loo, I spent the entire day and got the following nuggets.

> *At her debut bash, Dina Von Rillerbach's dance card was filled with the name Adam, scion of the super rich Moses Sterlings …*

> *Camilla, former Mrs. James Von Rillerbach and mother of the delightful Dina, tied the knot with polo pro Buzz Fortman at a private ceremony in the Hamptons …*

Spotted: the tantalizing trio, Dina Von Rillerbach, Bunny Lonegan and Sheila Waldron, cavorting through the Greenwich Village club scene … Rumors have it … former society sweethearts Buzz and Camilla Fortman are splitsville …

Which society girl has become jazz singer Georgia Valentine's new pet? Hint: DVR …

Date line, April 15, 1946 … Dina Von Rillerbach, chaperoned by mother Camilla, sailed on the Queen Mary on the first leg of their Grand Tour …

So it seems Bernice was right.

The other time period I searched was May 1 to 17, 1963, the day Georgia entered the hospital to the day of her death. I found these comments:

The recently divorced Camilla Fortman's new "friend" is a pal of the Riccio family, owners of a string of casinos …

Attention, jazz lovers, Georgia Valentine entered the Metropolitan Hospital with a mysterious infection …

Jazz fans are incensed over the Big Bad FDA searching the very sick Georgia Valentine's hospital room …
Jazz diva Georgia Valentine is planning to write a tell-all, making some people very, very nervous …

Jazz songstress Georgia Valentine died mysteriously of what authorities are calling a drug overdose …

Mitchell was tweeting fifty years before Twitter was even invented, and, though he was a purveyor of gossip, his comments were based on facts. It wasn't hard evidence, but considering we were dealing with a fifty-year-old crime, it was the closest I would get. He'd provided the dots, and now it was up to me to connect them.

Writing a tell-all? What did that mean? Was she planning to write her biography when she was sick in the hospital? Mitchell's line "making some people very nervous" jumped out at me. If she were writing a book and if she was planning to reveal her secrets as well as her gripes, I can think of some people she would have made "nervous," Maurice, Morey Stein, and Dina, just to name a few. Could the threat of a book been a motive to get rid of her?

I felt tired although all I had done was sit on my rear and search the Internet. My mind was on overload. I had too much information to sift through.

Chapter 46

I WAS NAKED, *standing at the apartment door, trying to hold it shut. A dark-haired man, unshaven and unkempt was trying to get in. I was pushing as hard as I could, but the chain was giving way. The screws were loosening. I pushed and pushed, but he was stronger. It was a matter of time before the door would open. His eyes met mine, his narrow and determined, mine wide and frightened. My phone rang but I couldn't move to pick it up. It rang again. And again.*

I woke in a sweat, breathing hard. I'd fallen asleep on the couch. I reached for the phone and mumbled my name.

"Casey, it's Nick. Did I wake you?"

"No, no. How you doing, Nick?" I didn't want to tell him I'd been asleep. He was on Pacific Time and didn't know I was three hours later, at midnight.

"I got that information you wanted."

I was wide awake now. "Yes?"

"The health inspector is taking bribes from Tony Lombardi."

"You sure?"

"Yeah, saw him at Tony's club and leaned on him a little. Believe me, I'm sure."

Nick had his own methods of getting information. I didn't ask him what he meant by "leaned on."

"I'm not surprised. Tony has wanted to buy Dee's club for a long time. She's not ready to sell, and even if she were, she'd never sell to him."

"Yeah, he's a bastard."

"Does Tony know you've found out?"

"No, and this inspector dude won't tell him either. You can count on that. Do what you want with it."

I didn't ask him what he did to ensure the guy's silence.

"Okay, great, Nick. I'll take it from here. What's the tab?"

"Nothing. I figure I owed you one. I'll get you next time."

We hung up and I sat back and thought a minute. I knew something about Tony he didn't want anyone to find out. And he wasn't aware I was sitting on this info.

All I had to do was make a call. But, first, I poured myself a glass of wine. I sat down in my easy chair, took a sip of wine and put a call into Tony at his club.

When he came to the phone, I let him have it. "Tony, this is Casey McKie, you know, Dee's friend?"

He interrupted with some bullshit comment, but I cut him off. "Never mind the crap. I know all about your plan to get Dee to sell the club, but it ain't gonna work."

He began to blubber about not knowing what I was talking about. I interrupted him again.

"Cut the crap, Tony, or should I say Ralph?" He was dead silent. "Yes, I know your real name and that you were Little Louie's boy back in Chicago. So, back off, leave Dee alone and I'll keep your real identity to myself. Understood?"

I could barely hear his mumbled "Yes."

"And if you ever try anything like this again, I'll expose you so fast you won't know who the hell you are. Capiche?"

He mumbled something. If people knew his real background, he'd be finished in North Beach. Now he was Tony Lombardi, respected owner of Tony's Bar and Grill in North Beach, San Francisco, one of the coolest places anywhere. But if people knew that he'd once been a member of the Little Louie's mob and had to get out of Chicago, he'd lose status so fast, he'd get the bends.

Now to let Dee know the good news. I called and got her, but her voice sounded lethargic. I hope she wasn't asleep at nine o'clock in the evening.

"Hey, Dee, got some good news for you."

"Yeah, what?" Her voice was toneless.

"You can schedule another inspection. I promise you'll pass this time."

She perked up. "Oh, yeah? How do you know?"

"'Cause I know why you didn't pass before."

I explained about the inspector being bribed by Tony.

Her voice got some life to it. "That motherfucker. Wanted to scare me into selling, huh?"

"Yep. But I straightened him out. He won't do anything like that again, I can assure you."

She laughed. "Girl, what did you do?"

"Well, you can say I made him an offer he couldn't refuse." The movie quote was too appropriate not to use.

Dee laughed again. "How'd you do that from New York?"

"I called in a favor from Nick Dasher, you know him, right?"

"Um um. I always thought you two would make a good couple."

It was my turn to laugh. "Me and Nick? No way. Besides, he's going with that underwear model."

"'You mean what's her name, the famous one?"

"Yeah, her."

Dee chuckled. "Yeah, you can't compete with that."

I laughed. "Thanks a lot. Anyway, arrange for another inspection and get that club opened. I'm gonna be coming home pretty soon."

Dee's voice went up a pitch. "When? You got the case solved? Did someone really murder Georgia?"

"Yes, and I'm that close to finding out who." I made a gesture with my thumb and forefinger, although Dee couldn't see it.

"Who? Tell me."

"Nope, you'll find out soon enough."

After some more bantering, we hung up with Dee in a considerably better mood. I realized how much I missed her and the club. I wanted to wrap up this case and get my ass home.

Chapter 47

As soon as I woke, my first thought was Georgia and her so-called book. I needed something concrete. First, I need to know if Georgia really intended to do such a thing. I wracked my brain as to whom to ask. *M.K. I bet she'd know.*

I called her and asked if I could come by.

I showered, dressed and headed for the subway station. I was beginning to enjoy this mode of transportation. It was so quick and sure as hell beat having a car. I guess we didn't have an underground in San Francisco because of all those hills. That would be a helluva lot of dirt to dig out.

One of the other great things about the subway was the music on the platforms. It was like a concert stage. Like today a young guy with a trimmed beard and nice clothes was playing classical pieces on a violin. It sounded terrific, the acoustics in the tunnel helping. I dropped a coupla bucks into his violin case. Smart kid, getting tips for practicing.

I greeted M.K. warmly. She smiled and waved me into the office area. She led me to the same room where we'd met before, but this time, she offered me coffee. She went into the next room, returning in a few moments with two steaming mugs.

Once we were seated, she said. "How can I help?"

"I heard that Georgia was thinking of writing a book and wondering if it was true. Did you find any kind of paper work, a contract or anything mentioning a book deal?"

She sat still a moment, probably doing a mental search, and then said. "You know, there was a book contract in her estate. It's dated a few days before her death. They gave her a thousand dollar advance."

That's where the roll of bills came from. I'd been wondering about that. "Who was the publisher?"

She gazed upwards a moment or two as she searched her memory. "Let's see. It was, um, yeah, RedDog Books, signed by, um, by Howard Roth. Yeah, Howard Roth." She smiled, pleased with her accomplishment.

I wrote the names in my notebook. I didn't have M.K.'s recall abilities.

I checked the time. If I hustled, I could make it to St. Patrick's in time to see Donna. I hope she was still going there every day. I thanked M.K., mumbled something about having lunch soon and hightailed it back to the subway.

I got to St. Patrick's a little before eleven and waited until Donna got settled before I walked up the aisle. Instead of sitting in the first row like I did before, I sat behind her.

I spoke very low, my head bowed as if in prayer.

"Donna, it's me. Casey McKie." She made a slight movement. "Please listen to me very carefully. I found out someone did go to the hospital that night. But I need your help to figure out exactly who it was."

She moved slightly.

"Can I come and sit beside you so we can talk?"

She nodded. I got up and moved to sit next to her.

She whispered. "What do you mean, you need my help?"

"I don't think it was a Sicilian who contacted you. I think it might have been a man who had a connection to them, but who was acting for a friend. But I need you to help me out."

She whispered. "How?"

"You said you saw a nurse that night. Was she someone you knew?"

"No, I thought she must be filling in. I never saw her before."

"What was she doing?"

"She was walking down the hall away from me, going in the opposite direction."

"Coming from the direction of Georgia's room?"

"Yes."

"Can you describe her? I know it was a long time ago."

"Oh, I remember. I remember everything about that night. I saw her face when she turned around. Let's see. She was older than me, prob'ly around forty, forty-five. And she was very pretty. I remember thinking she didn't look like a nurse, more like a woman you see shopping at Sak's, you know?"

"Yes, I know the type. Tell me this. Could it have been a man dressed like a woman?"

"No, no. Definitely not. I've seen men like that in Florida, you can always tell. Their shoulders. Their faces. No, it was a woman."

I told her I was close to discovering who it was and would let her know as soon as I did. If she could stop having to look over her shoulder all the time, it might make her life easier.

She whispered. "God bless you. All I want now is to enjoy my grandchildren."

I promised to get in touch with her soon and left.

It was a nice day, perfect weather to be outside, so I decided to walk to the theater. As I walked down the crowded streets, the buildings looming over me, I thought about how hemmed in I felt in Manhattan. The buildings were tall, the streets full of pedestrians and the streets jammed with traffic. San Francisco was a good-sized city, but it had an open feel, its hills creating a sense of space.

From my apartment in Chinatown, I could walk to Coit Tower and get a 360-degree view of the City. Or to the Embarcadero and get a view of the East Bay and the Bay Bridge. Or drive to the western edge of the city and walk on the beach. I never felt closed in. New York was a great city, no question about it, but I couldn't imagine living anywhere but San Francisco.

Like before, I waited at the stage door. I thought about how I'd approach Savoy. I didn't want her to walk out on me again. But before I had a chance to work up a strategy, the actors started coming out. Again, young people were waiting to get autographs from the stars. When Savoy walked out, I approached her.

"Hi, Ms. Davis, remember me?"

She gave me a baleful look. "I wondered when you'd show up again. I'm glad you did. I want to talk to you."

What was going on? The last time we met, she stormed out on me. Now she wants to talk. Maybe she wants to present me with a defamation suit.

"Well, good. I want to talk to you, too. Same place?"

She walked briskly and I followed. When we were seated with our coffee, she said. "How's your investigation coming along?"

I kept my gaze on her, wondering what she had on her mind. "Good, I'm almost finished."

Her eyes narrowed. "And what have you found out?"

I didn't know what game she was playing, but I answered with the truth. "I know Georgia Valentine was murdered. I know how and when it happened, and I have a good idea who did it."

Chapter 48

IF SHE THOUGHT I meant a member of her family, she gave no sign. "What will you do with the information?"

I knew what she was doing. She was fishing. "Well, there won't be a prosecution, if that's what you're worried about. Most of the people involved are gone. It would be difficult to prove anything."

I thought I saw a look of relief. "But," I continued. "I'm going to publish what I know in a prominent jazz magazine. I'm sure the story will spread from there."

She frowned. "Wouldn't that be irresponsible? You say you couldn't prove anything."

She was worried, all right. She must have discovered something. "I don't plan to name anyone."

Her surprise was apparent. "What do you mean?"

"When I'm certain who did it, and I'm close." I gave her a pointed look. "But I'm not going to mention the person's name. There's no reason. My objective, and that of the people who hired me, is simply to prove that Georgia Valentine didn't commit suicide."

"Why only that?"

I took a deep breath. "Because Georgia was a heroine to a lot of people, a role model, if you will, an inspiration." I took a sip of coffee. "Imagine being born to a poor black woman, barely a teen, who was unmarried and living in an unstable household. What sort of life could you expect?"

Savoy was staring at me. "You find you have a talent, a great talent, and you become very successful. People love you. You make them happy. You dedicate yourself to your art. But you still have personal problems, insecurities brought on by the life you were born into. You take drugs to make yourself feel better. You get into trouble over your habit and vow to quit. But you're not strong enough to resist. You end up killing yourself."

I gazed at Savoy. "What happens then to all the people who looked up to you, who said to themselves 'if Georgia can get off drugs and live clean, well, so can I'? What we wanted to do was change the lie in Georgia's history, to make sure she's remembered as a great artist, not as a drug addict who gave up on life."

I thought I saw tears in Savoy's eyes, but I wouldn't swear to it. She waited a moment, then spoke.

"I see. I'm sorry, I had you all wrong. I'm also the product of the life I was born into, although it was a lot different from Georgia's. But still I know what it can do to you." She sighed. "But I won't go into all that now. I was ashamed of how I acted when we last met. I didn't really know if what you said was true or not. I was shocked and reacted like my family would have done."

She paused to drink some coffee. "So I got out my mother's and grandmother's daybooks. Both of them were avid note takers. Well, even though they used abbreviations and cryptic language, I understood what they wrote. Yes, my grandmother was upset about Mother's relationship with Georgia, and I gather it was what you said, sexual. So she took her to Europe to break it up. Just as you thought.

"There was no more mention of Georgia in the daybooks until almost twenty years later until they heard she was planning to write a book. They read about it in the paper. My mother was preparing to get married, this time to a real catch, my father, and she loved him, too, and was worried a scandal would scare him off."

I didn't say anything, my heart racing, not wanting to interrupt.

She took a few moments, then continued. "My grandmother, Camilla, was at the time friendly with a man who was a little shady. He was involved in gambling casinos in New Jersey and I think he was connected to gangsters. But he had money and he spent a lot of it on Granny. That was more important to her than his character, I guess. Anyway, I gather from her notes, she told him about the book and how it might jeopardize my mother's marriage plans."

She looked down. "I think he may have been the one who -" she paused, then went on. "I think she made a bargain with him. If he helped with her, uh, problem, she would marry him. He wanted so much to be a member of what they call the upper crust."

She breathed a huge sigh of relief. I imagined telling this story was extremely difficult for her. I continued to look at her, not saying anything.

"So you have your culprit, my grandmother's gangster husband." She met my eyes, her lips forming a thin line. "Talk about dysfunctional families."

I could have let it go, but I couldn't. I had to tell her the truth.

"I appreciate your telling me this story. I know it was hard for you, but I have to be honest. It wasn't him. I have two eye witnesses who saw the person who did it. And it wasn't your grandmother's husband."

Her eyes opened wide, her jaw dropping. "What? But the notebook, I was so sure -"

Before she became too relieved, I told her. "The person who went into the hospital and injected Georgia with heroin was a woman. Judging by the description given by the witnesses, I'd say it was your mother."

I'd dropped a bomb, all right. Her shock was palpable, but she didn't bolt. She sat there calmly as she absorbed what I'd told her. Finally, she said. "Are you certain?"

I told her about the night nurse being threatened into leaving her station, the bribe, her quitting her job, moving away, and being afraid for her life all these years. How she'd seen an unfamiliar "nurse" that night coming from the direction of Georgia's room. I told her about Little Boy Barnacci driving a woman dressed like a nurse to the hospital and waiting for her and his description matching Dina's, though he didn't know who she was.

When I'd finished, she just sat there, looking stunned. I felt sorry for her. It had to be a shock to learn your mother was a killer.

Finally, she said. "I wonder why she did it instead of him."

"I think because a nurse wouldn't draw that much attention. Doctors are scarce in a hospital at night. Besides, she was experienced at giving injections. I read that she'd studied nursing at one time."

Savoy frowned. "Yes, that's right. She tried her hand at a lot of things. The sad thing is Granny had to pay by marrying that creep. She probably wanted to hush up the story for her own sake as well as my mother's. It would have destroyed her reputation, too." She sighed. "And Granny was miserable with him. Fortunately, he didn't live long. It seems odd to me that she would go to such lengths to hush up a homosexual affair. It's not that shocking."

"People's ideas about sex were a lot different then."

"Yes, that's true. But, you know, I'm not all that surprised that a murder happened. The more I learn about my family history, the more I realize how sordid it was. Infidelity, alcoholism, suicide, child neglect. You name it, my family's done it. Their values were totally screwed up. Status and wealth was all that counted. I rejected all that and am trying to live a different kind of life. Maybe that's why I gravitated towards acting, so I could take on new identities."

"You seem to be doing all right."

"Yes, I'm okay now. It took a while to get my head straight. But I love acting and I have a good marriage. No kids, though. I don't think I could handle that. Truth to tell, having money is a curse." She emitted a short laugh. "Now that we don't have any, we're a lot happier. But I must say learning that my mother –" she paused and looked around "- did what she did is going to take some getting used to."

215

I didn't answer. What was there to say?

We sat a little longer, then left to go our separate ways. I thanked her and reiterated my promise I would never reveal the true identity of the person who killed Georgia Valentine. I hoped she believed me. I'd lie to solve a case, but not this time.

She smiled at me as she walked away. "I destroyed the books, so there's no proof anyway."

Chapter 49

After I left Savoy, I felt like I was walking on air. The case was closed, or as closed as it was gonna get. I'd found out who'd injected an overdose of heroin into the most famous jazz singer in the world. I'd revised her history. I'd done what my clients had hired me to do.

Now I had to talk to Freddy. I spotted a bench and sat to make the call. He was my client and I owed him regular reports. At least I had something to talk about.

He was at home. After the usual pleasantries, I got to the point. "Freddy, I'm sure Georgia was murdered and I know who did it." He interrupted with some happy sounds, but I cut him off. "But, Freddy, the thing is I can't tell anyone about it, at least not name names. What I can do is report evidence proving she didn't kill herself but was murdered. But I can't say who did it. It will meet your objective of getting rid of the onus of suicide or overdosing accidentally. It will revise her history. She will be remembered as a great jazz singer and not as someone who took her own life. I hope that will satisfy you."

He didn't speak for a moment. "Of course it will. It's wonderful, Casey, but if you know who did it, why can't you say so?"

"Because that was the condition I agreed to in exchange for proof."

"And you can't go to the police?"

Little did he know I was collaborating with a cop, but I had to keep this to myself, since Ryan was breaking a lot of rules to help me. "No, the evidence would never hold up in court. Anyway, it's all hearsay and the guilty parties are dead. They couldn't be brought to justice no matter how many names I provided."

He sighed. "I see. But how will people know the story is true if it doesn't go to court?"

"It will appear in *JazzBeat* magazine, and the details are convincing. Once it's published there, it will spread, believe me. But, Freddy, you can't tell anyone just yet. You have to give me your word on that. People's lives are at stake."

That was a bit of exaggeration, but I had to make sure he didn't spill the beans until the magazine came out. I was assuming Aaron would accept the idea of an article. How could he not? This was the biggest story the jazz world had seen in a long time, maybe ever.

"I understand. It'll be hard to keep quiet, but I will. And, Casey, how can I ever -"

I interrupted him. "You can thank me after the piece comes out. I have more work to do."

"Okay. Did you remember my buddy is coming back the day after tomorrow? We'll have to get you somewhere else to stay. Maybe someone in the Society has an extra room."

"No, thanks, Freddy, I don't like to bunk with someone I don't know. I'll need a hotel room. Nothing fancy, just needs to be clean. And no bedbugs."

"Okay, I'll see what I can do. I'll catch you later."

It would be nice if I could wrap up the case before I had to move. But that would be a goddamned miracle. And I don't believe in miracles.

Then I called Aaron.

He was in his office. "Hey, how are you? I've been thinking about you."

"Got a few minutes to talk?"

"Sure. How's the case going?" I detected a change in his tone. I wondered why.

"That's what I wanted to talk to you about. I think I'll have it wrapped up in day or two."

He interrupted. "No shit. I'm amazed, but don't tell me you've discovered Georgia actually did kill herself."

"No, just the opposite. She was murdered. Deliberately. Intentionally." I added in case he didn't get my meaning.

"Christ, you actually know that someone killed Georgia Valentine?"

"Yes. And I have the evidence."

"Holy shit, who was it?"

"Before I get into that, I need to ask you, would you be willing to run an article on it?"

"Are you kidding? Of course I would, a big story like this, you're damned right I'll run it."

"Only one thing. I can't name names. I can tell the story, how it was done and why it was done, but not by whom."

"Why not?"

"Because in order to get the evidence, this is what I had to promise."

"Why?" He asked again.

"'Cause it would incriminate someone."

"Hey, wait a minute. Shouldn't murderers be incriminated?"

"The person I'd incriminate was not the murderer, but a witness."

"I see, but isn't that withholding the truth?"

"I'll tell the truth, just not all of it. Not the unnecessary parts. The objective was to tell the real story of how Georgia died. She'll no longer go down in history as someone who took an overdose to end her life. She'll be a triumphant figure rather than a tragic one."

"Okay, I guess that will have to do, but will people believe it if they don't know all the facts?"

"I think they will, if I explain why I had to withhold names."

He was silent. "I see. That makes sense, I guess. But I prefer the whole truth."

"I do, too, but, in this case, the alternative is no truth."

"Okay, I understand. You got it. I can get Dan Brennan to write it."

"Good, he's the person I was hoping you'd choose."

"When should I schedule it? When will you have it?"

"Can we make your next issue?"

"Let me see -" I heard him shuffle some papers. "Yeah, if you can get the outline to me in a couple of days. I'll bump what I have now and hold the space. And I'll get a cover photo. That's no problem."

"Okay, deal."

He paused. I could almost hear his brain spinning. "You'll be going home then, I suppose."

What was he about to say? I felt myself getting tense. "Yeah, 'course. I'm eager to get back."

"We haven't seen that much of each other. I -"

I knew what was coming, so I beat him to it. "It's okay, Aaron. I realized quite a while ago we didn't have a future together. Geography, for one thing. Religion, for another."

I heard the relief in his voice. "I didn't want you to think -"

"I didn't. Don't worry about it. You're gonna end up with some nice Jewish girl and live happily ever after."

'Funny you should say that. I've been seeing Ann Schulman, the flutist. Remember her?"

I laughed. "Yes, I do and I thought at the time that you'd be good together."

"No shit. You're psychic."

"Yep. Women's intuition, they call it. Okay, I gotta go finish up this case, so I can get you that article in time."

Well, that was it for Aaron and me. Easy as pie.

I had one more call to make, Donna Pellitano.

"Hello." Her voice was tentative, probably due to her constant fright.

"Donna, I wanted to tell you the good news. You don't have to be afraid any more. I know who murdered Georgia Valentine, and it wasn't the Sicilians."

Her voice tightened. "What are you saying?"

"I know who came into the hospital that night to give Georgia an injection. It wasn't a mobster. The man who called you was a friend of the murderer and he wanted to scare you."

"He did scare me. I been scared ever since."

"But you don't need to be any longer. The case is closed now. For good."

"What's gonna happen?"

"Nothing. Just a story in a jazz magazine." She started to protest. "Don't worry. Your name won't appear, although I will repeat the story you gave me. Without names. People will ask, but I won't tell anyone about you. I swear it. I'm not interested in revenge or even justice. I only want to prove Georgia didn't kill herself."

She started to sniffle. "I'm so relieved, I can't believe it. I been lookin' over my shoulder for all these years. And I won't ask who really did it. I don't want to know."

"I totally understand. But you can be proud of yourself. You've made an important contribution to the history of jazz."

Her voice was almost a whisper. "Well, thank you."

"And watch for the magazine *JazzBeat*. The story will be published there in a few weeks."

She was crying for real now. "Good, thank you, thank you. God bless you."

"You enjoy your grandchildren."

After we hung up, I sat there a few minutes, feeling good about Donna. But I couldn't forget she'd been living scared for half a century. Jesus.

I heard a dinging sound from my phone, two missed calls from Ryan. I returned his call.

"What's going on? I've been trying to get you. How's it going?"

I was almost singing. "Going great. I've finished the investigation. I know who killed Georgia."

"No kidding. You must be happy. I want to hear all about it. Wanna celebrate?"

"Damn right."

He laughed. "What do you want to do?"

"Go dancing. I want to go dancing."

Chapter 50

"THEY'RE BEAUTIFUL, Dee." I was admiring Dee's new stainless steel cabinets and counters. She was beaming. The club was open and business was booming. Everyone wanted to see the new kitchen, so Dee had a reopening party that included a tour of the space where customers weren't allowed.

I was happy to learn she'd changed the menu. She'd served the same six dishes for as long as I can remember. The new menu consisted of six different items, cheeseburger and fries, a filet steak with baked potato, spaghetti with meatballs, Chinese chicken salad, fish tacos, and a fruit and cheese plate, each one honed to perfection. She wasn't out to refine people's culinary tastes, she said, just give 'em what they wanted. And make sure it was tasty.

She hadn't, however, changed the music schedule. Like always, she had big band on Monday, Open Mike on Tuesday, two nights featuring herself, and week-ends reserved for out-of-town artists. Sunday was dark. She went to church, sang in the gospel choir and had lunch afterwards with friends.

Dee seemed to have regained her energy and I was no longer worried about her continuing to run the club. She'd brought in Sonny as her assistant. Sonny had managed the Take Five club after Milton Brown died. It was a smart move.

Harry walked into the kitchen. "She's back, our own Miss Marple. We missed you, didn't we, Dee?"

Dee put her arm around my shoulders. "Damned right."

The club's waitress Rae and bartender Willie had also come into the kitchen and were hovering over me.

It all got to be too much for Dee. "Okay, gang, let's take the party out of here. We gotta keep this kitchen spotless, you know."

We went into the club, Harry and I to his favorite table in the corner, Rae and Willie to their respective tasks, while Dee stayed in her new kitchen to talk to Angelo, the chef, probably critiquing the new menu.

After we were comfortably seated, Harry said. "So how the hell did you solve this cold case?"

I laughed. "Very carefully." Rae brought our usual drinks, a Campari and soda for Harry and a white wine for me. "You can read the *JazzBeat* article when it comes out. It'll explain everything."

Harry threw his arms out in supplication. "Come on, I can't wait that long. Give me the highlights."

Harry had such a pleading look, I couldn't say no. "Okay, just the main facts."

He leaned forward in anticipation.

I took a deep breath. "First, I managed to get the names of the people who knew the most about Georgia's death, her nurse, the cop who investigated the death scene, and the drug agent who directed the search of her hospital room before she died."

"And?"

"I found out Georgia had been sedated and couldn't have easily injected herself. The drug agents lied about a nurse reporting Georgia had drugs in her room, and the detective who came to the scene hated both drugs and black people."

Harry was smart enough to understand the implications of what I'd said. "So there was a rush to judgment. They concluded she'd injected herself despite evidence to the contrary."

"You got it."

"So how did you determine who did it?"

"I looked at who had motive. It turns out Georgia was planning a tell-all book, and at least two people were worried, her manager, who was afraid she'd tell how he'd been cheating her, and a person who was worried Georgia would reveal an indiscretion. Then there was Georgia's husband, Maurice, who would get her money if she died, not to mention the drug czar whose job was in jeopardy because of the hospital room search."

Harry's blue eyes were gleaming with interest. "Four suspects. Good grief. So how did you figure out which one was guilty?"

"Well, the husband wasn't going to get any money 'cause there wasn't any to get. And the manager's mob family didn't have any interest in putting a contract on Georgia, and the drug czar, well, he simply didn't have it in him to commit murder."

Harry thought a moment. "So that leaves the person who'd committed the indiscretion. It must have been a doozy."

"Yes, it was, for that time. No one would think twice about it today."

Harry rubbed his chin. "Not adultery, not shocking enough. Not drugs. Rape of a minor?"

I laughed. "No, although Georgia had been raped when she was underage, but the culprit had been long gone by this time."

Harry's eyes rolled upward, "Let's see. What's another shameful crime? Incest? Sex with animals?"

I laughed. "Nope."

"Gay sex?"

"Yep, that's it. Georgia had a lesbian affair with a very prominent society woman when they were young."

"Good grief. Gossip columnists would have pounced on that story like a tiger on a helpless deer." He frowned. "Doesn't seem a strong enough motive for murder, though."

"You have to consider the times. In those days, a story like that would ruin a person. You've heard about how Ingrid Bergman, you know, the actress in 'Casablanca', was barred from the United States after she got pregnant by a man who wasn't her husband?"

"Yes, I did hear that. I heard Congress passed a law about it."

"Yeah, a law, imagine. And don't forget the lengths gay movie stars took to keep their lifestyles secret."

"Yes, true. With sham marriages and the like. We've come a long way since then."

Harry took a sip of his drink. "So the murder was committed by a famous woman in order to keep her lesbian affair from going public."

"Yes. To people like her their standing in society is the most important thing in their lives. They go to great lengths to gain it and to keep it."

Harry's questioning eyes met mine. "Who was the woman? Have I heard of her?"

I shook my head. "I promised silence in exchange for the truth. So I can't say her name. Not even to you."

"Dammit, I'm dying of curiosity. But won't you be pressured to reveal it?"

"Yes, I'm sure I will be. People will discredit the story because of the lack of names, but that's too goddamned bad."

"Do you think the public will accept the story anyway?"

"The right ones will. When they know the circumstances."

Harry frowned. "But some won't."

"I know, but to hell with them."

"You've revised history. Not many people can say that."

"Maybe, but all I care about is that people will remember Georgia Valentine as a great jazz singer. Not as someone who killed herself with drugs."

Harry grinned. "Here's to you." We clinked glasses.

We fell silent. I'd returned from New York last night and been welcomed like a hero. You'd think I'd won the Olympics or something. Even though the *JazzBeat* article wasn't out yet, the story of Georgia Valentine being murdered had been leaked. I was being credited with solving a long held mystery. Did Georgia Valentine kill herself or was she murdered?

I wasn't stupid, and I knew that when the article was published, I'd get plenty of blowback over the lack of factual information. Did I care? Hell, no. The last thing on earth I wanted was fame. Celebrity was a pain in the ass, as far as I was concerned. If nothing else, this case proved it, seeing how the quest for celebrity screwed up the Von Rillerbach family.

After my meeting with Savoy, I'd gone dancing with Ryan and ended up moving in with him until I left. Talking about solving a murder case was a turn on, so after we talked over the case, had dinner and danced, we were, as the song goes, in the mood for love.

I stayed three more days, meeting with Aaron and Dan, working out the details of the *JazzBeat* article, and getting to know Ryan. I didn't know where it would go. I wasn't thinking that far ahead.

Right now I was looking forward to hearing Dee. It'd been too long. The trio launched into her intro music and we all turned to watch her stride to the stage. She was wearing her usual red, this time a low-cut, full-length gown I hadn't seen before. She looked smashing.

She stepped to the microphone and smiled at the audience.

"Tonight we're paying tribute to the great Georgia Valentine."

The audience broke into wild applause. She looked straight at me and launched into one of my favorite songs.

"God bless the child that's got her own."

About the Author

JOAN MERRILL IS the CEO of the production/talent management company, Saying It With Jazz. She has represented several jazz vocalists and worked as a video and radio producer, having produced the video documentary, *Saying It With Jazz*, fourteen shows for NPR's *Jazz Profiles*, and four shows for Smithsonian/PRI's *Jazz Singers*.

Merrill produced three CDs under her label, Saying It With Jazz, *You Don't Know Me* with Rebecca Parris, *Well, Alright!* with Nancy Kelly, and *"Que Sera! Celebrating Doris Day"* with Kristi King.

Merrill also created the tribute website, carmenmcrae.com.

She is currently producing the musical revue, "Que Sera! Celebrating Doris Day" featuring Kristi King.

For more information, go to sayingitwithjazz.com, joanmerrill.com and QueSeraTheMusical.com.

Ms. Merrill lives with her family in the Northwest.

Made in the USA
San Bernardino, CA
28 April 2013